*For every child in the Los Angeles foster care system,
and all the caregivers, social workers, attorneys,
CASAs, and other advocates who fight every day to
improve their lives*

M. G. HENNESSEY

the
Echo
Park
Castaways

**HARPER**

*An Imprint of HarperCollinsPublishers*

Also by M. G. Hennessey
*The Other Boy*

Library of Congress Cataloging-in-Publication Data

Names: Hennessey, M. G., author.
Title: The Echo Park castaways / M.G. Hennessey.
Description: First edition. | New York, NY : Harper, an imprint of
    HarperCollinsPublishers, [2019] | Summary: After going on a quest across
    Los Angeles together, Quentin, Vic, Nevaeh, and Mara, four very
    different foster children, realize that they have become a family.
Identifiers: LCCN 2018025432 | ISBN 9780062427694 (hardback)
Subjects: | CYAC: Foster children—Fiction. | Adventure and
    adventurers—Fiction. | Brothers and sisters—Fiction. | Asperger's
    syndrome—Fiction. | Attention-deficit hyperactivity disorder—Fiction. |
    African Americans—Fiction. | Hispanic Americans—Fiction. | Los Angeles
    (Calif.)—Fiction.
Classification: LCC PZ7.1.H464 Ech 2019 | DDC [Fic]—dc23 LC record
    available at https://lccn.loc.gov/2018025432

Typography by Michelle Gengaro-Kokmen
19 20 21 22 23   PC/LSCH   10 9 8 7 6 5 4 3 2 1
❖
First Edition

*For every child in the Los Angeles foster care system, and all the caregivers, social workers, attorneys, CASAs, and other advocates who fight every day to improve their lives*

# ONE

## QUENTIN

"Are you ready to go, Quentin?"

I shake my head. The lady's mouth pinches at the corners. Her lips are pink, too pink, and her face is brown even though she's white, which means she *does not apply proper sun protection, at least thirty SPF!* The lady's lips match her sweater, and she is wearing white pants even though it is April. *No white pants until Memorial Day—without rules, we have chaos.*

"No white pants," I say helpfully, because this is useful information for everyone to have.

"What?" She gives me a funny look. "Did you forget to pack something?"

I shake my head again.

"Okay, then. We really have to go, Quentin," Pink Lips Lady says, looking at her phone. She is always looking at her phone, even though as a grown-up she should know that is very rude, especially when other people are there. *No phones at the table especially; dinner is for nice conversation.*

Pink Lips Lady tries to take my backpack, but I hold it tightly because it is my responsibility.

She makes a face and sighs. "Do you really want to stay here, Quentin? Trust me, the next place is much nicer."

I look around. This room is not nice. It is too cold and the furniture seems dirty and I do not like it at all. None of my things are here, not my bed or my R2-D2 clock or my comforter or my desk with the matching chair. I want to go home, where *everything has a place.*

"Home," I say.

"It's a lovely home," she agrees. "Let's go there together."

She holds out her hand. I do not take it, I do not like touching, and besides you are not supposed to even talk to strangers. But when Pink Lips Lady walks toward the door, I follow her.

"This is going to be fun!" she says to her phone, but I do not think it will be fun at all.

# VIC

Here's the thing almost no one knows about me: I actually work for the government. See, when I was just a kid (well, I'm technically still a kid, but you'd never guess my age. Go ahead, guess. All right, I'll tell you. I'm eleven. But I'm totally mature for my age, right? And that doesn't even count my mad ninja skillz. . . .)

Okay, so I was telling you about my super–top secret job. I mean, I shouldn't even be sharing this, obviously (top secret, right?), and it's that old "If I tell you, I have to kill you" thing, but I swear I won't kill you. I figure you can be trusted with something this important.

Anyway. When I was ten, I noticed that a black sedan was tailing me home from school every day. Of course, as soon as I realized this, I took some serious countermeasures (and, like, totally lost them). It became a kind of game for me: spot the sedan, then see how fast I could get away from it.

And it's a good thing I did, because it turns out that was actually a test. And I passed! So a few weeks later, I walked out of school and found a guy waiting for me. Now, normally I wouldn't go near some creepy guy in a suit who was lurking outside a school (Logan Street "Elementary," even though it goes through eighth grade). I was planning on shaking him, too, but then he said the magic words that got my attention.

"Victorio Quintero," he called out. When I stopped, totally shocked that he knew my name, he added, "I know where your father is."

So I went with him. I know what you're thinking: *Vic, that's nuts! Stranger danger! Even someone with a twentieth-degree black belt shouldn't go off with a crazy white dude!*

Listen, I completely get where you're coming from. But if your father had vanished on a secret mission four years ago, then someone showed up and said they knew where he was, you'd want to hear what they had to say, right?

Besides, I wasn't a total idiot. I stayed close to school, just going a little way down the block with the guy and keeping an eye on that sedan in case it came any closer.

"You know I can outrun you, right?" I said.

That made him laugh, and he said, "Vic, my boy, that's just one of the many fine qualities we've observed in you over the past few weeks." Then he pulled out a brand-new iPad and showed me all these videos. There were clips of me practicing my parkour (you know, leaping off benches and climbing buildings like Spider-Man), whipping around my nunchucks, and totally killing the obstacle course I set up in our backyard.

"What are you, some kind of creep?" I asked suspiciously (because who takes videos of a kid unless it's their own?). I was getting ready to scramble up the chain-link fence and vault over the other side in a perfectly executed maneuver when he showed me the only video that mattered: my father, in a prison cell. The image was dark and kind of greenish, like it had been taken by a night-vision camera. My dad was tied to a chair, with a blindfold over his eyes. He'd grown a shaggy beard and was a lot skinnier, but I could still tell it was him.

"Let him go!" I yelled.

"Easy, now. We're not the ones holding him prisoner," the guy said, trying to calm me down (and looking a little scared).

"Then tell me where he is!" I demanded, my hands balling into fists. Seeing my dad like that made me want to rush right out and save him.

"He's in El Salvador."

My heart totally sank when he said this. I mean, it made sense, since my dad was originally from there, and had only gone back because the country needed him. "Sometimes we have to make hard choices, son," he'd said, clapping a hand on my shoulder as a single tear slid down his cheek. "But I swear on your mother's grave, God rest her soul, I will return as soon as it's safe."

Even though I was only seven years old then, and I was bummed that he was leaving, I totally understood. My dad's a hero, and heroes have a calling.

I'd thought he'd be back by that summer, though, and now it was four whole years later. So seeing that video of him in a prison cell in El Salvador explained everything. He'd been captured! It wasn't his fault!

I started to storm away, and the guy hurried to keep up with me. "Where are you going?"

"To El Salvador," I said through gritted teeth.

"That's far away, Vic," he said. "How do you plan on getting there?"

"I'll figure it out," I said.

"I can help you."

I stopped dead. "Why would you help me?"

"Because I believe we can help each other." The guy put a hand on my shoulder and leaned in, looking into my eyes. "You're a remarkable boy with a very special skill set. A hero, just like your father. And if you devote yourself to serving this country, I'll make sure he's rescued."

"What do you want me to do?" I asked suspiciously.

That's when he told me all about this new government task force they were forming, made up of kids like me. The government finally realized that kids are practically invisible; people will say all sorts of crazy stuff around them, figuring they're harmless. So who should be doing the spying? Kids, that's who! Which is precisely why the government formed the Delta Elite Eagle Corps (we call it the DEEC), made up entirely of kids like me who are even better at stuff like fighting than most adults.

To be honest, pretending to be a normal fifth grader has been tough. I have to sit through boring classes, when I could be sparring at the DEEC center instead, learning the ancient secret art of wushu kung fu from Master Shei. But my boss (the guy from the sedan, Commander Baxter) insists that my cover is perfect: after all, who would suspect that a foster kid in LA was really a spy?

I'm getting antsy, though. I've done a whole bunch of missions now, breaking up Russian and Chinese spy rings, even totally destroying a terrorist plot and saving, like, a ton of lives. But still, according to Commander Baxter, every attempt to rescue my father has failed. It's getting to where I'm going to have to insist that next time, they take me along. Otherwise, I'll threaten to quit, and they can't afford that; I'm their best agent, the other kids even nicknamed me Ace because I'm just that good.

Hopefully, it won't come to that. I'll give them one more month, then I'm going after my dad on my own.

After all, he'd do the same for me.

## NEVAEH

"Oh my God, what is he *doing*?" Jada squealed.

I turned just in time to see Vic running along a park bench. He tried to do a somersault off it, and ended up face-planting in the grass on the other side. I rolled my eyes. "Being an idiot, as usual."

"I'm okay!" Vic yelled, popping back up. The knobby knees poking out from his basketball shorts sported some new raw scrapes, but otherwise he looked fine. Thank God, because I was not in the mood for another trip to the ER.

"Be careful, loser!" I reprimanded him. "If you get hurt again, I swear you're on your own."

"Like I need your help." Vic scoffed, but he returned to the sidewalk.

"*So* embarrassing," Jada said sympathetically. "Man, and I thought my brother was bad."

"He's not my brother," I mumbled as Vic fell back in step behind us. He didn't stay there long before jumping onto the concrete wall that separated the sidewalk from the park. He held out his arms to the sides like he was walking a tightrope, mumbling his usual monologue: "Parkour means training not just your body, but your mind. Just an instant of lost focus can mean the difference between life . . . and death. . . ."

I sighed. Jada laughed and said, "It sucks that you're stuck with such annoying kids."

"Totally," I agreed. "Could be worse, though. I had this one foster brother who was always lighting fires—"

"Yeah?" Jada was tapping away at her phone again.

"Never mind," I said, annoyed. Half the time I was jealous of the kids my age with fancy phones, and the other half I was creeped out by it. It seemed to turn them into zombies. I wasn't sure I'd ever want one—not that it was even an option. I was lucky to get a new pair of jeans for Christmas last year.

"Hey, Nevaeh!" Vic always talked a little too loudly, like his volume button had been set wrong at birth. "Tell Mrs. K I might miss dinner. I've gotta go on another mission. Top secret, need-to-know only."

"Ignore him," I groaned.

"Sure," Jada said. "OMG, you should see this video Aliyah just sent, it's totally LOL. Want to hang out after you drop him off?"

I shifted my backpack to my other shoulder. "Can't. Mrs. K is working late."

"Oh, right," Jada said sympathetically. "I swear, it's like you're the mom over there."

"Tell me about it," I muttered. We called our foster mother Mrs. K because Kuznetsov was hard to pronounce. The past few months, Mrs. K's work shifts usually started before we got out of school, and ended way past our bedtime. Which meant that I was basically in charge of raising Vic and Mara.

I first moved in with Mrs. K almost a year ago, after being pulled out of one of the worst foster homes ever (and believe me, after living in seven over the past eleven years, I'm an expert). So when I walked into Mrs. K's relatively clean house in a decent neighborhood and saw a couple of sweet-looking younger kids, it was a huge relief. As a bonus, the local school was good, too; if I kept my grades up, I'd qualify for one of the best high schools in the city next year.

But that all depended on Mrs. K, and at the time, she was clearly a mess. Honestly, I was surprised that our caseworker, Ms. Judy, hadn't yanked the other kids out of the house, but that's the LA foster care system for you: they were so desperate for places to put kids, they accepted pretty much anyone as a foster parent.

Not that Mrs. K was bad; she was nice enough, and there was always food in the fridge. But she barely got out of bed for anything except work, and she kept muttering about foster kids being more trouble than they were worth now that her husband was gone.

So I set out to change her mind. It started small. I'd get up early to make breakfast and pack school lunches. That seemed to make her happy, so I offered to make dinner, too. Before I knew it, I was shuttling Vic and Mara to and from school, nagging them to do their homework, and getting them ready for bed.

I don't know any other eighth grader stuck with all that. But the more that I helped out, the less Mrs. K grumbled about quitting the foster system. She still spent most of her time in bed when she was home, but she wasn't missing work anymore, and she occasionally even made it downstairs for dinner.

As long as I kept her happy, I'd have a roof over my head until it was time for college. And after that, when I headed off to UCLA on a full scholarship, well . . . maybe Vic would pick up the slack. Regardless, he and Mara wouldn't be my problem anymore.

Although it would be a lot easier if he weren't so annoying. I frowned as Vic nearly tripped an old lady when he dodged in front of her.

"Apologize," I barked at him.

"Sorry, ma'am!" Vic yelled at her.

She muttered at him in Russian and kept toddling down the sidewalk. There were lots of Russians like Mrs. K around here—lots of other immigrants, too. Echo Park was still one of the poorer neighborhoods in LA, although it was generally pretty safe, and lately I'd seen a lot of flashier young people hanging around the new cafés and restaurants. Mrs. K was always grumbling about how they had no respect for the neighborhood. But old people always hated anything new. And as far as I was concerned, an overpriced café was a lot better than a pawnshop with steel gates and graffiti. Echo Park definitely felt a lot safer than some of the places I'd lived, and it wasn't like the neighbors were exactly neighborly anyway. Everyone pretty much kept to themselves, which was fine by me.

I grabbed Vic's arm to stop his constant motion and asked, "Did you take your meds today?"

His eyes slid to Jada and he frowned. "What, my superpower pills?"

"Yeah, those," I said, repressing a sigh.

"Nope. Ran out."

That explained why he was even more hyper than usual; without a regular dose of his medication, Vic acted like someone had just pumped him full of a candy store's worth of sugar, topped off with energy drinks. "We'll stop at the drugstore after we get Mara."

"I still don't get why she's at a different school," Vic said. "I mean, if she was at Logan, I could keep an eye on her."

"That's above my pay grade," I muttered, although I'd wondered the same. It would make my life a lot easier if we didn't have to walk an extra half mile to her bus stop, but Ms. Judy had insisted that Mara finish third grade at her current school to "lessen the negative impact on her." It was hard not to feel a little resentful about that; my other caseworkers had no problem yanking me out of schools every time my placement had changed. Ms. Judy was still too nice because she was new.

We stopped at the corner where Mara's bus pulled in every day at quarter past three. Mara barely talked, which was a big plus in my book. She also did what she was told without being asked a dozen times, which made her easier to handle than Vic. He'd become distracted in the middle of getting dressed and end up wandering the house in shorts and a single sock until I threatened to drag him to school like that.

I checked my beat-up watch: 3:10 p.m. We were right on time, despite Vic's dawdling. I leaned against a brick wall flanking a yoga studio. On the other side of the plate-glass window, a bunch of super-skinny women were contorting themselves on brightly colored mats. Yup, the neighborhood was definitely changing. Three storefronts down the street were under construction; one sign proclaimed, *Fresh Organic Produce Coming This Spring!*

"Did you hear? They're putting in a Sephora!" Jada said. "How awesome is that?"

"Awesome," I agreed, even though the chances of me ever walking into a fancy makeup store were slim to none. Sephora was replacing a little market that had been totally run-down, but the owner would give us candies sometimes when she was in a good mood. I wondered what had happened to her.

"So, which superhero is he now?" Jada asked, watching Vic talk into an invisible receiver while holding his ear.

"No more superheroes, I guess he outgrew them. Now he thinks he's a superspy." Vic existed in his own dreamworld, employing what Ms. Judy called "coping mechanisms." It didn't hurt anyone (except himself occasionally, thanks to all his acrobatics), so I let it slide. Of course, it meant he was pretty much a pariah at school, but that didn't seem to bother him. Or if it did, he didn't complain about it. Not that we ever talked about anything other than what we were having for dinner; we shared a house, that was all. My job was to make sure he was still alive and relatively whole when Mrs. K got home every night; anything beyond that was his business.

Jada's phone buzzed. Checking the screen, she broke into a grin. "Aliyah's parents are working late again; she wants us to come chill."

"Have fun," I said mechanically.

"You could come later, maybe?"

I let myself imagine it for a minute: watching a dumb movie with a bunch of other eighth graders, eating snacks and joking around. *It's not worth it*, I reminded myself. "Maybe next time."

"Yeah, sure. Next time," she said knowingly.

Jada threw a wave over her shoulder as she walked away. I felt a pang, watching her go. She and Aliyah had been spending a lot of time together lately. Aliyah was pretty and popular. She lived in a huge house with a TV the size of a movie screen, or so I'd heard; lots of kids hung out there after school. I couldn't blame Jada for preferring that over spending time with crazy Vic and silent Mara. I'd do the same if I had a choice.

*A little over four years until college*, I reminded myself. *Then medical school.*

"Get down," I snapped at Vic, who was trying to climb the brick building next to the bus stop. He threw me a look, but lowered himself to the ground.

"I gotta practice my mad skills, Moneypenny," he boomed.

"I told you to stop calling me that." A few of the waiting parents were smiling to themselves, which made me want to crawl into a hole. I really needed to get his prescription refilled.

Thankfully, Mara's bus pulled up. She was the last kid to shuffle off, a tiny Latinx girl with enormous eyes and a mop of black curls. I eyed her hair; it was a little long. I should probably trim it after her bath tonight.

"*¿Bueno?*" I asked, which was pretty much all the Spanish I knew.

Mara nodded. Grabbing her hand and avoiding the sadness in her eyes, I said briskly, "Then keep up. We have to stop at the drugstore for Vic."


# QUENTIN

This is not my home. It is not even my street.

This house is tall and narrow and the windows are

dark and it is brown. The paint is peeling, and everyone knows that means the owners are not doing *proper upkeep and maintenance*. Mommy makes sure our white paint is always nice and fresh; she has men climb ladders to redo it every third summer (*like clockwork!*), except she missed last summer because she was *otherwise occupied*.

The front door opens and a woman comes out. She stays on the porch and looks down at us. Mommy says that when the corners of people's mouths turn down either they're sad or maybe just not very nice, and those people *are to be avoided*.

The porch lady's mouth looks like that, so I decide to stay in the car. Pink Lips Lady opens my door and undoes my seat belt and says things in the same voice Mommy used to use with our dog, Mr. Pebbles (*who has gone to a better place!*), but I cross my arms because she is not my mommy and also not a doctor or a police officer, so I don't have to do what she says.

Pink Lips Lady steps back and frowns. She says something to Porch Lady, and both of them come over to the car and talk at me but I don't listen; instead I slide down in my seat and look at my backpack. There is a new black mark above Yoda's head that was not there before I got into this dirty car, and I rub it with my finger but it will not come off. I will have to find a clean white cloth and get it damp with cold water and *dab it, don't wipe.* I look at the house again, but it does not seem like a place where there will be clean white cloths.

Pink Lips Lady sighs, and the sad lady goes back up to the porch.

If I stay in the car, maybe Pink Lips Lady will take me to my real house. We have a stack of cloths there in the cabinet next to the washing machine, and there is also a *Magic Wand Stain Remover That Is Safe for Washable Fabrics and Removes Stubborn Stains in Seconds!* This is a stubborn stain, and I know that Mommy will not be happy when she sees it, but it is not my fault, because of the dirty car.

Our Camry is always clean on the inside and smells like a forest, unlike this car, which smells like old fries and cigarettes like the people outside the hospital smoke that *are terrible for your health and you should never, ever do that!*

Now that I notice that, I realize that I would like to get out of this smelly car. But if I do that, I have to go into the brown house, and I do not know how that will smell yet. I know they won't let me stay on the sidewalk because pretty soon it will be getting dark and *bedtime is at seven thirty, you're a growing boy and need your sleep!* And I cannot sleep on the sidewalk and I cannot go home because I tried that already and Pink Lips Lady just came to get me with her smelly car.

Three people are coming down the street—a tall black girl and two smaller kids with lighter skin. They slow down when they see the lady on the porch. They are all carrying backpacks—the tall girl has a navy one, the boy green, the small girl pink. The tall girl also has a white plastic bag.

"Hi, Mrs. K!" Tall Girl says. "Why aren't you at work?"

Porch Lady says, "I stay home to welcome new family member."

But her voice is not nice as she says this, and she is looking at me. I want to explain that I already have a family, I have Mommy, she's just *currently indisposed*, but I keep my mouth shut.

The three kids stare at me. They are not smiling or frowning, and they do not say anything, either. Then the boy says, "Where's he going to sleep?"

"In your room, Vic," Porch Lady answers. "On top bunk."

Bunk beds are dangerous. An average of thirty-six thousand people a year are hurt on bunk beds. I will not sleep on a bunk bed in this brown house. I will especially not be on the top bunk, where the *risk of serious injury* is much higher.

"What's he doing in the car?" the boy asks.

"He's a little shy," Pink Lips Lady says in that same

Mr. Pebbles voice. "Maybe you can help us convince him to come in?"

I burrow deeper into the seat. But Tall Girl comes over and says, "Come on. You're just making it worse for yourself."

She sounds tired. I shake my head. I want to start hitting it—that might make them go away—but Mommy says to *never do that; it only makes things worse, it doesn't fix the problem,* so I make my hands into tight fists instead. My sharp fingernails dig into my palms, and that feels nice and calm.

Tall Girl leans in and looks at me and says, "I know it's tough. But trust me, it's okay here."

I look at her. Her skin is smooth and dark, and her hair is all twisted around itself. I like the girl's hair. I like her face, too: even though she is not smiling, she is not frowning, either. I get out of the car. She reaches her hand out, but I do not take it.

"He doesn't really like to be touched," Pink Lips Lady says. I can tell by her face that she is happy I am out of her car. I want to tell her that for just $17.99 the Sunrise Car Wash in Torrance will clean it *inside and out, 100 percent hand-wash when it's time to shine!* They even use a special spray that makes it smell like new. But instead I walk slowly up the stairs to the house. Porch Lady nods to Pink Lips Lady and opens the door for me. I hesitate for a second, because it is dark inside, but then I remember that *there's no reason to be afraid of the dark; it's just like closing your eyes but for longer,* and so I hold tight to my backpack and go in.

# TWO

## VIC

"Is he slow or something?" I asked, staring at the new kid while we all ate dinner. At first I was totally pumped—I mean, finally, another man in the house! Hanging out with a bunch of girls all day can be a drag, especially for an alpha male such as myself. I wasn't totally pumped about sharing a room, obviously, because it would be harder to sneak out on my top secret missions. But so far the kid hadn't said a word, not even to ask for salt, even though it was tough to get through Mrs. K's "meat loaf surprise" without it.

"Shh!" Mrs. K said sharply, glaring at me. "He has the Asperger's."

I couldn't help it; I started cracking up. "Ass burgers? Like, burgers come out his *ass*?" Her accent made it sound even funnier.

Mrs. K swatted me on the shoulder for using a bad word, even though she'd used it first. Between that and how hard I was laughing, I ended up sucking a piece of meat loaf down the wrong pipe, which kicked off a coughing fit. Nevaeh had to smack me between the shoulder blades to keep me from choking.

The kid didn't even seem to notice that we were talking about him, though.

"What's that?" Nevaeh asked, looking nervous. I could tell she was wondering if maybe she'd have to do something extra for Quentin, like change his diapers or something. And maybe she would—that would explain why the word "ass" was part of it.

"It means Quentin sometimes has a hard time talking to people. He don't understand always how to act." Muttering to herself, Mrs. K added in her annoyed voice, "Judy didn't say it was this bad."

Nevaeh looked relieved. I was a little bummed, though. I mean, I didn't have time for friends anyway, between school and top secret missions. But it might've been nice to have someone to talk to. I watched the new kid mechanically scoop meat loaf into his mouth: he chewed, swallowed, and cut off another piece. It was kind of weird, like he was spending the exact same amount of time on each bite. Maybe he was actually a robot, some sort of top secret prototype that the government was working on. That would be cool. I wondered if there was a way to check. . . .

Mrs. K said, "So be extra nice. Yes?"

I nodded. Mrs. K was cool, even if her English was terrible, which was weird since she'd lived in Los Angeles for, like, twenty years. She spoke enough to get her point across when she wanted to, though, believe me. And her work schedule made it easy for me to slip away when duty called. I kind of suspected that Commander Baxter had chosen her to be my foster mom for exactly that reason. Maybe she'd been, like, a Russian spy in a previous life, and after she defected, they set her up in a safe house.

I eyed her. Mrs. K was seriously old, like fifty, and always wore lumpy sweat suits. Which was kind of a great disguise, if you thought about it. No one would look twice at her, either.

"Take your pill," Nevaeh reminded me, passing it across the table.

I obliged, swallowing it down with milk. Last fall I stopped for a while, convinced they were part of a plot to stop my superpowers, but then something bad happened at school, so now I take them. Better to keep everyone happy, right? And if choking down a pill every day accomplished that, then why not?

"Hey," I said, leaning over toward the new kid. "Our names are kind of similar, you know that?"

"Vic and Quentin?" Nevaeh snorted.

"My *last* name," I threw back at her. "Quentin and Quintero, get it? Maybe Quintero even means Quentin in Spanish. You hear that, man? We're practically brothers from another mother!"

I held out my fist for him to bump, but he just stared at it. *Definitely a robot*, I thought. His clothes were the biggest clue: he had on khaki pants and a pale blue shirt buttoned all the way up, like a dorky grown-up had dressed him. When she dropped him off, Ms. Judy huddled in the kitchen for a long time with Mrs. K explaining stuff—a lot longer than usual with a new kid. Hopefully this "ass burgers" thing wasn't something you could catch; I kind of wanted to ask, but if it turned out to be a dumb question Nevaeh would give me her death glare.

Mrs. K hadn't really eaten much of her food, either.

"The meat loaf is great," Nevaeh said. "Really yummy."

I rolled my eyes; let's just say that when Mrs. K cooked, it wasn't exactly a special treat. Not that Nevaeh was much better; she pretty much just made hot dogs and mac and cheese. Mrs. K got a funny look on her face, like she was about to cry, and said, "Was my husband's favorite."

"Oh. Well, it's awesome," Nevaeh said in her fake-cheerful voice.

She nudged me under the table, so I mumbled, "Yeah, awesome."

I dragged another bite through ketchup and licked it off. I hated when Mrs. K got like this. I mean, her husband died, like, five years ago, before I even got here. Shouldn't she be over it by now? You didn't see me sobbing into the meat loaf about my mom, even though I obviously still missed her.

Mrs. K's shoulders had dropped, and she'd kind of sunk into herself. Mara was looking at her, wide-eyed, and Nevaeh was biting her lip. The new kid was still just sitting there ignoring all of us.

Mrs. K sighed and said, "Long day."

"I can do the dishes if you want," Nevaeh said quietly.

That made me snort—I mean, she pretty much always did the dishes anyway, who was she kidding?

Nevaeh shot me a look as Mrs. K said, "Thank you, Nevaeh. I think I go to bed now." Looking up, her eyes landed on Quentin, and she frowned. "I should—"

"I can help him get settled," Nevaeh interrupted. "You should rest."

Mrs. K looked grateful. She got up and patted Nevaeh's arm, then shuffled upstairs.

Nevaeh looked at the stack of dirty dishes in the sink and sighed.

"Well, you asked for it," I pointed out.

She threw me a nasty look as she got up from the table and said, "You could help for a change, you know."

"I always help!" I said.

"Yeah, right. You always get Mara to clear for you."

"Not true," I said, pulling my plate back from where Mara had already stacked it on top of hers. Mara smiled at me when I put a finger to my lips. She's a good kid. When she first moved in, I tried to teach her English, but she didn't seem that interested, and I don't like to speak Spanish anymore unless I have to, like on undercover missions. "I'm even clearing Quentin's. Dude, you done?"

He didn't answer, so I took his plate away even though there were still a few bites left.

"You want help with the dishwasher?" I offered.

"Can't risk you breaking another plate," Nevaeh said, which was totally unfair because that only happened once—okay, maybe twice—and besides, the way she was slamming them in right now, she'd probably break a few, too. "Take Quentin upstairs and get him ready for bed."

"He's not a baby," I pointed out.

"I want my baby back, baby back, baby back ribs," Quentin suddenly said out of nowhere.

We all looked at him. He'd picked his backpack off the floor and was holding it in his lap, staring at the spot on the table where his plate had been.

"That was him, right?" Nevaeh said doubtfully. "Is he still hungry?"

"If he is he's out of luck, because we don't exactly have ribs," I said.

"Right." Nevaeh turned off the tap. "Just make sure he brushes his teeth, okay?"

"You got it, Money . . ." Off her look, I said, "Just kidding. C'mon, Quentin." When he didn't move, I tapped the table in front of him and said, "Time to jet, you feel me?"

I grabbed the duffel bag that Ms. Judy had left by the kitchen door. When the new kid saw that, he got up and followed me, so I guess "ass burgers" didn't mean he was totally out of it. I led him through the house, giving the grand tour along the way. "This is the living room, we can go in there, but we're not supposed to bring food or else Nevaeh totally freaks out. And that's the dining room, which we seriously only use, like, twice a year on holidays. And that's the door to the backyard. I've got an obstacle course set up out there if you ever want to use it."

Quentin didn't seem to be paying much attention, but I kept going anyway. "Nevaeh is cool. And did you know her name is 'heaven' spelled backward? I think that's pretty awesome, but she doesn't like it when I tell other people. My name, of course, means 'victorious,' because I'm the hero of all mankind. Mara is cool, too, but she doesn't talk much. Hey, do you speak Spanish?"

I wasn't really expecting him to answer anymore, so I just kept explaining stuff as we climbed the stairs.

When we got to our room, I checked the piece of tape at the bottom of the bedroom door: still intact, which meant my cover hadn't been blown. Not that it would be, because I'm super careful, but still, I'm always relieved when it hasn't been tampered with. Mara went into our room once, and when I came home and saw the wrecked tape I came pretty darn close to grabbing my "go" bag and bailing. Luckily, she confessed to the crime when she heard me yelling about it. No harm, no foul. *Just stay out of my room*, I'd reminded her.

Our *room now*, I thought. This was definitely going to put a crimp in things. I gestured to his backpack. "Yoda, huh? So you like Star Wars?"

Without looking at me, he said, "Fear is the path to the dark side."

"Right." I nodded. I wasn't a big Star Wars fan myself, but Yoda was cool. And, man, for a little old alien guy, he could fight. "So anyway, this is our man cave. Which bunk do you want?"

Speaking of Star Wars, Quentin was eyeing the bunk beds as if they were a couple of Stormtroopers brandishing blasters. My stuff was still on the top bunk; I'd chosen that specifically to keep a clear line of sight to both the door and window.

Boy, was I happy when he slouched and sat on the edge of the bottom bunk. He looked pretty relieved, too.

"Shoot," I said, shaking my head with fake dismay. "I was really hoping for the bottom bunk. But since I've been sleeping up there for, like, three years, it's cool. The desk is mine. You can use it, but don't look in the drawers, on pain of death. You feel me?"

He looked at the desk. I could tell he wasn't going to answer, so I kept going. "Awesome. And you can call me Vic. Just so you know, sometimes I head out kinda late. It's totally fine, though. Mrs. K knows all about it."

It was hard to tell if he was even listening. Quentin sat on the edge of the bed like he was stranded on top of a cliff or something. Mrs. K had remade it with clean sheets and a ragged blanket that I recognized. *Mario's blanket*, I thought, before quickly pushing that away.

"Hey, I could call you Q!" I said, snapping my fingers. "You know who that is?"

He just kept staring at the desk.

"He's this super-smart guy who makes all James

Bond's weapons and stuff. And your name starts with Q, so that could be your new nickname!"

Nothing. I shrugged. "All right. I gotta do some homework, then we brush our teeth, and it's lights-out by twenty thirty. That's eight thirty, in case you don't know military time."

Fully dressed and still wearing his shoes, Q rolled onto the bed and turned to face the wall, curling into a ball around his backpack.

I gotta admit, seeing him like that gave me a little pang. Even if he was a robot, he definitely seemed unhappy about being here. I wanted to say something, but I flashed back on what Commander Baxter had drilled into us: *The first priority is saving yourself. Civilians are secondary.*

So instead, I went over to the desk and pulled out my math homework.

## NEVAEH

It was past eight o'clock by the time I got Mara bathed and ready for bed. Then I had to remind Vic (repeatedly) to do the same. The new kid was already asleep, as far as I could tell: he was lying down fully clothed, still wearing his shoes. *But he's in bed, and that's all that matters*, I told myself. I really didn't have time to deal with whatever his issues were. I still had to do my own homework.

I ignored Mara's light snores as I worked at the desk in the corner of our room. I liked this time of night. The drone of Mrs. K's bedroom TV was a little annoying, but other than that, it was nice and quiet. I started with algebra, then finished the worksheets for social science. We were learning about Rome, which based on my ragged textbook seemed pretty much the same as our world now: If you were rich, life was easy. If you weren't, not so much. I was willing to bet that back then, kids like me weren't being fed grapes off platters, that was for sure. And if something happened to your parents, you were basically on your own—good luck to you.

Pretty much like the foster care system, at least as I'd experienced it. Most foster parents fell into one of three categories: religious nuts, people doing it for the money, and elderly folks like Mrs. K who either never had kids of their own, or who wanted to replace theirs when they moved out. Of those groups, I much preferred the old people.

Of course, I'm kind of a unique case. A lot of kids don't stay in the system long to begin with: their parents work out their problems, or another family member decides to take them in. But my mom died when I was two years old, and as far as anyone knew, she was my whole family. So unlike Vic, I've never thought that someone might come for me. When I was really little, I used to dream about getting adopted, like Orphan Annie or something, but that was unlikely after you turned six. So instead, I came up with a plan. If no one was going to rescue me, then I'd rescue my own self.

What a lot of people don't realize is that the foster care system can kick you out when you turn eighteen. And I mean the *day* you turn eighteen, whether you've finished school or not. Luckily, I have a late birthday, in August, so I'll only have to find a place to stay for a month or so before college starts. UCLA has a special scholarship program for local foster kids, so it shouldn't be too hard for me to get in. If I stacked my courses and went to summer school, I could graduate from UCLA in three years. I'd need to stay at the top of my class to earn a full scholarship to a great medical school. Four years of medical school (it was almost impossible to finish early—I'd checked), then three years of a medical residency. And then I'd (finally) be a full-fledged doctor. Helping people for a living would be nice, but honestly I cared most about never having to worry about the cost of anything, ever again.

I decided to finish my English homework in bed. I worked hardest on math and science, because if you wanted to become a doctor those were the most important subjects. But this year, English had been pretty cool, too. We were reading this book *Holes*, about a kid who got sent to what was basically a prison work camp. I could totally relate; my last placement was with a family who'd taken in seven foster kids. The foster mom and dad didn't even bother learning my name: they marched me straight into their garage, which was filled with sewing machines on rickety desks. They told me that whenever I wasn't in school, I would be helping with their "hobby": making dog beds that they sold online. And if I didn't finish at least five dog beds a day, I wouldn't get dinner. I spent three months there. I'd sleep, go to school, come home, make the dog beds, eat dinner, and fall into bed exhausted every night.

Then one of the other kids nearly cut off his finger while helping with their other "hobby," carving floating ducks for hunters. They didn't even take him to the hospital, just slapped a few Band-Aids on it and sent him to school. When the kid fainted from losing so much blood, Child Protective Services finally swooped in. The foster parents were arrested, and all seven of us were taken back to the "Welcome Center," this awful place where they keep foster kids between placements. I hated it there. We were assigned to plastic-covered bunk beds that smelled like pee, the food was disgusting, and there were a lot of fights between the older kids after lights-out. I basically never slept at all whenever I got stuck there.

The kid in *Holes* had it even worse, though; he was forced to dig these giant holes in the middle of the desert with a bunch of other kids, and the people in charge were the worst bullies imaginable. I was almost at the end of the book, and I was really hoping the kids would end up getting their revenge. Of course, that would never happen in real life: If this were a true story, the kid would do his time, and then leave and never think about the other kids again. And they wouldn't think about him, either, and no one would ever report the grown-ups who made them dig holes, and it would just go on and on and on. . . .

That's why I liked reading fiction. It was nice to get a happy ending for a change, even when it was totally unbelievable.

It was hard to concentrate, though, because I could hear Vic's relentless chatter through the thin walls. I mean, seriously, that kid never shut up. I rapped once on the wall, hard enough for him to hear, but not loud enough to alert Mrs. K. Silence fell.

I imagined the poor new kid, spending his first night in a strange house, trapped with a boy who wouldn't stop blathering on about ridiculous spy stuff.

"Sweet dreams, Quentin," I whispered, then caught

myself. *He isn't my problem.* I picked my book back up
and found my page.

## QUENTIN

The boy in the dangerous top bunk won't stop talking.
I have never heard anyone talk so much. At our house,
Mommy and me only talk when there is something to
say.

But this boy is like the night we forgot to turn
off the TV and when we woke up in the morning the
people were still talking about *breakthrough fourteen-
minute max interval workouts that challenge your
whole body, including your core!*

I pull a pillow over my head, but even through that
I can hear him. He is talking about spies and missions,
and I have no idea what any of it means. All I know is
that someone has made a *serious mistake*, like the time
Mommy brought a blanket home from the store and it
turned out to have a hole in it and right away she got
on the phone to explain to them about their serious
mistake. Like that.

Finally, he stops talking and I can hear him breathe.
It reminds me of when Mr. Pebbles used to lie at the
foot of my bed and sleep: His chest went up and down
and I could hear the air going in and out. Loud, but not

bad. Sometimes his leg would start twitching, too, but the loud boy stays very still.

Loud Boy said he was going outside, and I hope he does. It will be much quieter then.

But I lie there and wait, and he does not leave.

# THREE

## VIC

Okay, so I might've drifted off for a bit. I mean, at first I was *pretending* to sleep, waiting until the new kid zonked out so I could exfiltrate without him noticing.

But somehow, I ended up falling asleep myself. I know, it's hard to believe that someone like me could make such a rookie mistake. In my defense, Commander Baxter says we all slip up from time to time.

Anyway, *something* woke me. I jolted up, whacking my head on the ceiling (stupid top bunk! Maybe I should've switched to the lower one after all). I sat there for a second, breathing hard, ears cocked for the slightest sound, braced to react. . . .

I realized after a few seconds what was throwing me off: the new kid wasn't rocking anymore. I mean, seriously, for a while there it had been like an actual earthquake, the whole bed was shaking like some sort of carnival ride. Hard to believe I'd managed to fall asleep through all that, but now, it had stopped.

I peered over the edge of the bunk: empty. Maybe he was just using the bathroom?

I waited a minute, then decided to investigate. Mrs. K's house wasn't exactly spacious. Our room was at the top of the stairs. The bathroom was down the hall to the right, next to the girls' room (which was two square feet larger than ours, which I know because I measured it once. Not that I'm complaining, since ours is on the fire escape, which makes it easier to slip out). Mrs. K's (much larger) "master suite" was in the middle.

The bathroom door was open, the light was out. I tiptoed over and peeked in, just to make sure: empty. So I eased my way downstairs, careful to avoid the boards that creaked, and checked all three rooms. It was completely dark.

Robot Boy was gone.

I grabbed an apple out of the bowl on the kitchen counter and sat at the table munching it thoughtfully. It wasn't unusual for a kid to run away, especially on the first night. This one, though—I didn't have high hopes for his survival, you know? I mean, a guy like me could make it out there indefinitely; between my street smarts and my training, it would be NBD (no big deal).

But this newbie was a different story. Echo Park

wasn't the worst neighborhood, but it wasn't exactly the best, either. Especially after midnight. I chewed slowly, mulling over the problem. I could just go back to bed; after all, it wasn't like he was my responsibility. Tomorrow morning, Mrs. K would report him as a runaway, then DCFS would track him down (if he survived) and drag him back to the Welcome Center. Because here's one important fact about Mrs. K: she doesn't tolerate runaways. If you left her house, even for just a night, you weren't allowed back in.

That was the thing that tugged at me: it had been just the three of us for almost a year now (Mara came last September, Nevaeh in October). I'd been wondering when the other bed would be filled; Mrs. K liked to stay at capacity, since the government paid roughly a grand a month for each of us. I was actually kind of surprised that it had stayed open this long, but after what happened with Mario, I guess Mrs. K wasn't totally keen on taking in another boy. And the rules said she couldn't stick a girl in a room with me, even though I'd be a total gentleman, obviously.

So if Q washed out, someone else would probably show up soon. And that, more than anything, was the best argument for going after him. It was pretty obvious that Quentin the crying ass-burger robot wouldn't be a problem, but what if his replacement was older, or nosier, or worse?

I sighed and shook my head, then got up to throw the apple core in the trash. "All right, kid," I muttered. "The cavalry is coming."

## NEVAEH

"Nevaeh! Hey, Nevaeh!"

Someone was shaking me. Irritably, I turned over and mumbled, "Go 'way."

"You gotta get up!"

I opened my eyes. Vic was bent low over me, his greasy hair hanging in my face. I swatted it away and hissed, "What are you doing? Go back to bed!"

"Can't," he said, straightening. "We've got a mission."

I glanced at the clock and had to repress the urge to scream. "It's one thirty!"

"Exactly," he said, leaning back far enough to make the ladder groan. "He won't last much longer out there."

"Who?" I stifled a yawn. My mind was already spinning into gear, loading my daily to-do list. I had a Spanish test today, and needed to finish my math homework during free period—

"The new kid!" Vic said impatiently in his overly loud voice.

"Shh!" I checked the lower bunk to make sure

Mara was still asleep. "What, he took off?"

Vic nodded. "About ten minutes ago."

"Why didn't you stop him?"

He cocked his head to the side and gave me a funny look. "We're kind of wasting time here. Are you going to help me find him or what?"

"Or what," I said automatically, flipping over to face the wall and pulling the blanket over my head.

"Suit yourself," Vic said, adding a dramatic sigh for good measure. A couple of seconds later, I heard our bedroom door click shut, then the sound of him going downstairs.

Of course, now I was wide awake; going back to sleep would be hard, maybe impossible. There was a quaver through the floorboards as the front door closed.

*Not my problem*, I told myself. Uselessly, because I was already picturing someone luring that idiot Vic into a van; all they'd have to do was promise some sort of ninja adventure. And Quentin had "victim" written all over him.

If something happened to them, DCFS would come down hard on Mrs. K. And then she might quit the foster program, which would mean that all my hard work would've been wasted.

*That's why you're doing this*, I told myself, pulling on a pair of shorts. *It's not for them, it's for you.*

# QUENTIN

It is very dark out. Back home there are streetlights, so even in the middle of the night it is a safe place to walk, but here many of the streetlights are broken and that is a sign that *things are going to heck in a handbasket.*

When I reach the corner, I stop and check the sky. Today is April eighth. Jupiter is the most visible star right now (not a star, though—a planet!), and it will be moving west/northwest. I find it right in the middle of Cancer the crab (*Snap, snap!* Mommy always says, pinching me, but not too hard).

We live in Torrance, which is south/southwest of Echo Park (so far I have not heard any echoes, or seen a park, so this is a terrible name). If I walk away from Jupiter, past the brown house again, I will be going in the right direction. Toward home. Toward Mommy.

I walk back toward the brown house, checking over my shoulder to make sure Jupiter stays behind me. Last time, when I left the other place, the stars were all gone before I could find Torrance. I sat on the sidewalk to wait for dark, but people kept stopping and talking at me and then the police came and then Pink Lips Lady drove up in her smelly car and took me back. I do not know why she keeps taking me places other than home, but it means that I must *rely on my own resources.*

So tonight I left as soon as Loud Boy fell asleep. This time I will not let Pink Lips Lady find me. I will get home and Mommy will open the door and I will fall asleep in my own bed with no bunk on top.

As I pass the house again, I walk faster. My backpack is heavy, so I hold the straps tight and continue to the end of the block and am about to cross the street (*looking both ways—safety first!*) when someone yells, "Hey!"

I do not look back. I cross the street quickly, then glance back to check Jupiter. Loud Boy is running toward me. He is wearing pajamas and sneakers and he is frowning. I cross the street as fast as I can walk, but he catches me and grabs my arm.

"Hey, Q!" he shouts in my face. I try to get my arm back, but he holds it tightly. "Good thing you didn't get very far. C'mon, we gotta get back."

I shake my head—*no, no*—but he does not listen, he just holds my arm, and then Tall Girl is there and she is yelling too, and suddenly it's too loud and I need to block it out, need to make it stop. I know it is bad, but I start hitting and hitting and hitting and it feels good, it feels so much better, all their noise goes away. . . .

# FOUR

## VIC

"What's wrong with him?"

Nevaeh looked freaked-out, too. "What did you do?"

"Me? Nothing!" I said. "I just told him we had to go back. He didn't lose it until you showed up."

She threw me a look. I crossed my arms and glared back at her. Meanwhile, Q was basically beating himself up. He was making weird noises, too, kind of panting and hiccuping at the same time. It reminded me of the Hulk changing—like Q was fighting it but couldn't stop it. I half expected the kid to swell up and turn green, but instead he collapsed on the ground and started rocking back and forth.

"That's better, I guess," Nevaeh said.

I eyed him doubtfully; sure, he was quieter, but he

also didn't look like he'd be walking any time soon. I asked, "What now?"

"How am I supposed to know?" Nevaeh asked, throwing her arms up. She was wearing a pajama top and shorts, and her hair was piled on top of her head. I couldn't help it, I started cracking up. I mean, we looked totally ridiculous, standing outside in our pajamas in the middle of the night.

"It's not funny!" Nevaeh yelled, but that just made me laugh harder.

Except she was right: it was about to get a lot less funny.

Like I said, Echo Park is pretty safe, especially our street. Most of our neighbors are old Russian people like Mrs. K, and while no one is exactly friendly, they usually nod when you walk past. They spend most days working on their gardens or sitting on their porches. It's nice, actually.

But at night after all the old people go to bed, it changes, and not in a good way. There's a street a few blocks away where people race cars and do doughnuts; the pavement is scarred with tire circles. On the block behind ours, there's a house that's quiet in the daytime, but at night, guys hang out on the porch drinking and swearing and sometimes fighting; Nevaeh made me promise to never go near it. And a few months ago, we heard something that I could've sworn was gunshots, even though Nevaeh scoffed and said it was just fireworks. Of course, Echo Park isn't half as dangerous as the places where I do my missions, but it's not Disneyland, either.

So at the sound of an engine, my ninja senses kicked in and I stopped laughing. There was a car cruising up the block toward us. It was all tricked out with lights around the license plate and shiny rims—the type that cost a lot of money. The car slowed as it came closer, and the passenger-side window slid down to reveal a guy wearing sunglasses even though it was pitch-black out. He looked Nevaeh over and made kissing noises, loud and gross.

Someone else in the car said, "That's nasty. She's just a kid." I got a knot in my throat. I could totally handle these guys if I had to, but that would blow my cover, you know? And there were at least three of them in the car, which made it tricky. But I had to protect Nevaeh. I started breathing hard, my mind spinning while I tried to figure out what Commander Baxter would want me to do.

Nevaeh's jaw had gone tight. She grabbed Q's arm and tried to yank him up, hissing, "Move!" The car was really close now, only ten feet away. I grabbed his other arm, trying to be helpful.

Q started making this high shrieking noise, like we

were murdering him or something. We both let go at the same time, and he slumped back to the ground, rocking again.

"Crap," Nevaeh muttered.

"Yeah," I agreed. We were only a couple hundred feet from home, but we couldn't exactly drag him there screaming; he'd wake up the whole neighborhood, including Mrs. K.

Although maybe that wouldn't be so bad; it would probably make these guys take off. But Mrs. K would be mad, and maybe we'd all get kicked out. I could tell Nevaeh was thinking the same thing; she was biting her lip and looking toward the house.

"You cool, man?" the guy in sunglasses called out.

"He's fine," I said. My voice came out shaky.

Sunglass Guy muttered something, and the car peeled off with a roar. I heaved a sigh of relief; they were gone, at least for now.

"Quentin!" Nevaeh said in a low, urgent voice. "Get up!"

I bent down and leaned in: Q was muttering something, over and over. I listened for a minute, trying to make it out.

"He's saying 'mommy,'" I reported.

"Great." Nevaeh puffed out her lower lip. Crouching down to our level, she said in a low, soothing voice, "Quentin, honey, you can't see your mommy tonight."

He stopped rocking and went very still. A low rumble from down the street—the car was circling back, the headlights flared a block away. Nevaeh and me exchanged a look—that wasn't good, and we both knew it. "Maybe . . . maybe we could take you to see her," I offered desperately.

Q tilted his head up. His eyes were bloodshot, his cheeks puffy and red. "See Mommy," he repeated in a hoarse whisper.

"Sure," I said quickly. "We'll go see her together. Right, Nevaeh?"

She shook her head furiously at me, but we had to get this kid inside. I thought of Mario again, and that galvanized me. I put my hand on my heart and said, "Here's my solemn oath. If you come back with us now, I will reunite you with your mother."

Nevaeh rolled her eyes, clearly annoyed, but it worked. Slowly, Q got to his feet. Staring at the ground, he plodded back up the block toward our house. We fell in step behind him.

I heard the car pull even with us. "Remember, sugar. We got space for you anytime!" Sunglass Guy called out. The others laughed. We both started to walk faster, without daring to look at them.

Nevaeh muttered, "A solemn oath? Seriously?"

"It worked, didn't it?"

"You shouldn't have lied to him," Nevaeh said.

"I didn't lie!" I said. "I gave my word, and I'm a man of honor. So yeah, I'm going to help him see his mom."

She stared at me for a second, then shook her head and laughed. "You're crazy."

I ignored her, because obviously she had no idea what I was capable of. Finding Q's mom would be the easiest mission I'd undertaken in a long time—after all, it wasn't like she was in El Salvador, right? It would take a week, max. And then I'd get back to my own quest: rescuing my dad.

I pictured him tied to a chair in a cell somewhere. I wasn't about to admit it to Nevaeh, but when Q said "mommy," it got to me. I understood how he felt. As we hurried to catch up to Q before he did something dumb, like slam the front door, I felt a surge in my chest. It was a noble quest, worthy of my skills. Q was lucky he'd found me.

## NEVAEH

Mrs. K was already downstairs making eggs when my alarm went off. That was so weird that for a minute I panicked and thought maybe she knew about what happened the night before, and this was our last meal before she kicked us all out.

But no, she was just putting on a bit of a show

for Quentin's first day. I tried not to feel resentful as I picked at my eggs; I was pretty sure I hadn't gotten a hot breakfast on my first morning here. I certainly hadn't gotten many since, not unless I'd cooked them myself.

It was wasted on him anyway, though. Quentin sat there staring mutely at his untouched plate, the dark circles under his eyes indicating that he hadn't slept much, either. He already had his Yoda backpack on, and it pushed him so far forward he was practically falling off his chair.

My eyes felt like they were filled with sand, and I couldn't stop yawning. Even Vic was uncharacteristically quiet. The only one who didn't look exhausted was Mara, who goggled at us while she mechanically shoveled food into her mouth. Mrs. K stood next to Quentin, frowning at his uneaten food. "You don't like eggs?"

Quentin didn't respond.

"They're really great," I said. "Perfect, right, Vic?"

"Huh? Yeah, awesome." Vic's plate was already empty—when Mrs. K turned back around, he reached over and speared a clump of eggs off Quentin's plate with his fork.

"Stop that!" I hissed.

"What? He's not going to eat them," Vic said. "Are you, Q?"

No answer. I sighed; I didn't have the energy to make a big deal out of it.

Mrs. K's cell phone rang from the hall table. Mumbling, she dried her hands on a kitchen towel and shuffled to answer it. Mrs. K was taking Quentin to school to get him settled in, so we'd all have a ride for a change. I checked my watch and said, "Mara, we're leaving in ten minutes, okay?"

She nodded and got up to clear her plate.

Mrs. K's voice suddenly got louder. I exchanged a glance with Vic—it had to be work; no one else ever called her. A minute later, she appeared in the doorway looking upset.

"What is it?" I asked.

"I must work early," Mrs. K said. She waved an arm at Quentin. "But I promise Ms. Judy I take Quentin to school."

We all looked at Quentin. This was clearly a problem.

"You can't say no?" Vic asked.

Mrs. K shook her head. "No, Vic. You know my boss."

Her boss was a little guy with squinty eyes who always acted like we were there to rob the place whenever Mrs. K brought us in to buy clothes with her employee discount. Even though she'd been working at the store for more than ten years, he was always threatening to fire her. I'd found Mrs. K crying at the kitchen table more than once because of something mean he'd said. She'd told me that if she lost this job, she'd probably lose the house, too. And then we'd all be in trouble.

"I guess I could take him," I said doubtfully. "I mean, we're all going to the same school, right?"

"So weird that there isn't a special school for ass burgers," Vic muttered. "Like, one with buns on the outside."

He started snort-laughing at his own joke. I ignored him.

"Ms. Judy says there is special teacher, but not right away." Mrs. K was wringing her hands. "I need to go to office with him—"

"I can do that," I said. "If you drop off Mara, I'll take Vic and Quentin. Her bus stop is on your way anyway."

"You sure, Nevaeh?" Mrs. K asked uncertainly.

"Yeah, no problem," I said, trying to sound more certain than I felt. How big a deal could it be? I just had to get him to the office, and then someone would probably handle it from there, right? "We should go soon, though. Vic, get your shoes on and help Quentin."

"I have to do everything," Vic grumbled, getting to his feet and leaving his plate behind.

"Clear your plate!" I called after him.

"I already have a job!" he yelled back. "Remember?"

Mrs. K still looked conflicted. "I can go late to work—"

"It's fine," I said reassuringly. "Seriously. I got this."

"Good girl," she said, patting my shoulder as she went by. "Thank you."

I stacked the dishes in the sink and ran some water for them to soak. Then I leaned on my hands and closed my eyes. I could hear Vic banging around upstairs, Mrs. K's heavier tread across her bedroom, the lighter patter of Mara's feet. "Five weeks until school is out," I said in a low voice. "Four years until college."

"Learning today for a better tomorrow," a voice piped up behind me.

I turned around. Just like last night, Quentin was sitting there staring at the table as if he hadn't said a word. It was weird, the way he'd just blurt out random things. Probably part of his Asperger's. "We're leaving in five minutes, Quentin," I said. "So if you have to pee or anything, you'd better do it now."

The whole walk to school, Vic was talking a mile a minute, outlining his nutty plan for reuniting Quentin with his mom. I tuned him out. He *never* should've promised that. If Quentin's mom had really wanted him, she wouldn't have lost custody in the first place. DCFS didn't take kids away from great parents. I knew that from experience.

The bell was ringing as we approached the school's entrance. "C'mon, Quentin," I said. "We'd better hurry."

I started running for the door; first period I had Spanish, and every time I was late, Señor Garcia would totally humiliate me in front of the entire class. I'd barely gotten ten feet when Vic yelled, "Hey! Nevaeh!"

"What?" I whirled around. He was still at the front gate, tugging at Quentin's arm. Quentin had dropped to the ground and was rocking back and forth again, just like last night.

Vic yelled, "He's doing it again!"

I gritted my teeth; this was the absolute last thing I needed. I hurried back and bent down so that my eyes were level with Quentin's. He was blinking fast, like he was trying to hold back tears as he said, "No, no, no . . ."

"Quentin, we have to go to the office. It's okay, I'll stay with you the whole time."

"No, no, no . . ."

"I don't think he wants to go," Vic said helpfully.

I threw him a look. The second bell rang, meaning I was definitely going to be late for Spanish. Why couldn't anything ever be easy? I was half tempted to just leave them there, but Vic had a pleading look in his eyes, and something about Quentin got to me. He wasn't like us, not really. Vic and Mara and me were used to being on our own. Quentin obviously wasn't.

"Quentin, honey," I said, trying to sound calm and reassuring. "School's starting. We have to go in, like, now."

He raised his eyes to meet mine. There was real terror there, like I'd just announced we'd be carving him up for dinner.

"It's cool, man," Vic said, clapping him on the shoulder. Quentin flinched. "I bet they even put you in my class."

Quentin shook his head again. In a voice barely above a whisper, he said, "No school. Dangerous kids. Not safe. Better to learn at home."

I stared at him, perplexed. "Wait," I said, suddenly getting it. "Are you saying you've never been to school before?"

"Home," Quentin said. "Mommy."

"No way!" Vic exclaimed. "Dude, I am, like, so jealous. Do you have any idea how many missions I would've accomplished by now if I didn't have to come here?"

"Enough already, Vic," I groaned.

"What?" he said defensively. "It's true."

Quentin had squeezed his eyes tightly shut, as if he

was attempting to wish himself somewhere else.

"Miss Parker! What's going on over there?" Looking up, I saw Mrs. Colbourne, the yard lady, bearing down on us.

"This is our new foster brother," I said, gesturing to him. "He's, um . . . he's a little nervous. It's his first day of school, ever."

Mrs. Colbourne's face softened as she took in Quentin. "Hello, dear. What's your name?" Kneeling down, she put a hand on Quentin's shoulder. He flinched away and squeezed his eyes shut, rocking back and forth even faster.

"He doesn't like to be touched," Vic explained. "He's got ass burgers. His name's Quentin, but I call him Q."

"Where's your foster mother?" Mrs. Colbourne said accusingly, as if we'd done something with her.

"She got called in to work early. I promised to take him by the office, but . . ." I waved my hand at him helplessly. The third bell rang; class was starting.

"I can't believe they didn't set him up with an aide," Mrs. Colbourne said disapprovingly.

"Our foster mom said he'd get one soon, just not right away," I explained.

"Of course not." Mrs. Colbourne shook her head and sighed. "Budget cuts, I'm sure. Well, my nephew

**56**

is autistic. Maybe I can help." Lowering her voice, she said, "Quentin, I'm Mrs. Colbourne. No one is going to hurt you."

Quentin opened one eye and looked at her dubiously.

"There now, see? It's all okay, you're perfectly safe here. Can you get up? I promise not to touch you."

Awkwardly, Quentin got to his feet, pulling his backpack on again. He stared at the ground.

"Excellent, Quentin!" she exclaimed. "Why don't I take you into the office to get you squared away? Does that sound okay?"

Quentin didn't say anything, but he looked less terrified.

"Wow, Mrs. C. Nice," Vic said.

"Thank you, Mr. Quintero." As she led him toward the door, Mrs. Colbourne called back over her shoulder, "You two are already late. Better hurry!"

"Man," Vic said. "She's never that nice to me."

"Me either," I said, feeling a little resentful. The only time Mrs. Colbourne had ever spoken to me was when she yelled at us for running across the yard.

"Oh well," Vic said cheerfully. "See you later." He stopped halfway to the door and called out, "By the way, the planning meeting's at sixteen hundred. Don't be late!"

I hated it when he did that military time thing. "Planning for what?"

"For the quest, dummy!" He threw the door open and ran inside.

"I'm not doing your stupid quest!" I yelled back, but he was already gone.

I dragged myself to the door, feeling a lot older than thirteen.

## QUENTIN

I hate school. It is loud. The other children are loud, the bells are loud, everyone talks at the same time, and it never ends—it is just noise noise noise. I plug my ears, but the noise still makes it in. A lady stands at the front of the class and she just talks and talks and writes things on a big white board. At home, we don't have a big white board. We have a real computer with *educational guidelines and a special curriculum designed specifically to maximize my potential.* Mommy says it is much better than school, and she is right because no one can learn anything in all this noise.

Loud Boy sits next to me, and he is full of noise, too. While the teacher talks, he talks, whisper whisper whisper, until I want to start hitting again, but *we must not hit*, hitting is not good for heads, and my head is perfect and must not be touched, otherwise it might not be perfect anymore.

Real school is when Mommy and me sit at the computer and it is quiet and we can do math and science and history and no one else is there talking at us. We are learning about the Oregon Trail with a game of pretend. In the game it is long ago, and we have wagons and horses and cows and we are traveling a long, long way *for a better life*. And sometimes people get sick, or there is not enough food, so we have to decide whether to stop or keep going. And if you make the wrong decision, you die and have to start over. It is a great game. I almost never die, but Mommy does, all the time, and then she laughs (but not too loudly) and says that I have to take care of the hard decisions, she is no good at it. And I promise that I will, and she squeezes my arm and kisses the top of my head in the safe spot (a little to the right, above the ear) and she says I am her little man and she loves me more than anything.

This teacher will never say that. And I bet she has never heard of Oregon Trail; in fact, if she plays it she will die quickly from snakebite or dysentery or maybe just exhaustion from all that talking. And I will not help her; my wagon train will leave her behind.

Loud Boy says we are going on a quest. I have not been on a quest before, but maybe it will be like when Luke Skywalker and Han Solo save Princess Leia from Darth Vader. Loud Boy will help me save Mommy from the hospital, and that is almost the same because the hospital is a big building with many loud machines that breathe like Darth Vader.

I am ready to go on the quest. I have been very patient. I came to school and sat through all the noise and did not do the hitting and now I want to go back to Mommy and my computer and the Oregon Trail. I want to tell Loud Boy that, but he never stops talking, so I just sit and listen and try not to hit.

# FIVE

## VIC

Man, is Q lucky to have me around. I mean, this kid is lost with a capital *L*, if you know what I mean.

For example: at lunch, he didn't even know you had to get in line at the cafeteria. I had to drag him over or I swear he probably would've stood there staring at the food for, like, forever. And then he went for the sloppy joe—I mean, you never, and I mean absolutely, positively never ever, take the sloppy joe. I don't know what they put in there, but it's definitely not meat. I stopped him just in time and told Marcia (the lunch lady, who always sneaks me extra because she says I'm "charmin' like Marvin") that he was my new brother and I was showing him the ropes, so she gave us each an extra chocolate pudding, which was a total score!

Anyway, it's already clear that most of the planning for the quest will be up to me. Nevaeh is pretty organized, but with something like this, every detail is critical. The only problem so far is that Q-man isn't exactly forthcoming with details—he's still pretty much only said, "Mommy" and "home" and "baby back ribs" and once, weirdly, "wagon train," and I was like, *Yeah, I get it, dude, but maybe a few more deets would actually help us find your mom, you know? Like, is she in jail, rehab, or a deportation center?* (Those are all basically different kinds of jails, in case you didn't know that.)

I've seriously been grilling him all day, while Mrs. Cordero went on about commas and fractions and all that other stuff at the smartboard. But Q-man never said a word. I mean, I gotta say, this kid would probably hold up under some pretty intense interrogation.

Obviously, reuniting him with his mom is gonna be tough if I don't even know where to start looking. But I don't let that get me down. It wouldn't be much of a quest if it weren't hard, right?

At least he didn't freak out again. That would've been pretty embarrassing. The other kids steered clear of us, which suited me just fine. Q isn't exactly going to help me maintain a low profile, but he's strange enough that people are avoiding him instead of picking on him. At least for now.

When we got home, I put together a plate of cookies and brought them into the living room for the meeting

(I told Q we weren't supposed to bring food into the living room, but that rule doesn't really apply to me because I'm such an expert at not leaving a trace). At 16:10 (4:10 p.m.), Q and me were still the only ones there. He sat in his chair staring at an Oreo like it held the key to the universe or something. He was still wearing that darn Yoda backpack, too; it was kind of weird how he never ever took it off. Maybe he had a secret inheritance in there.

"Dude, what's in your pack?" I asked.

Q looked at me but as usual didn't say anything. So I kicked my heels against the chair legs and ate three Oreos to keep my energy up, then finally went to find Nevaeh.

She was in her room, working on homework as usual. Man, I'm so happy I don't have to worry about school, since I've already been assured that when I turn eighteen, I'll automatically become a covert CIA agent and will travel all over the world doing missions and breaking the hearts of gorgeous ladies. And how's math supposed to help with that?

"Hey!" I said, standing in her doorway—Nevaeh is kind of touchy about her space, ever since I broke her pocket mirror completely by accident when I used it to check if I was being followed.

"Back up a step; you're technically in the room," she said without looking up.

"We're waiting on you for the meeting!" I said. "Quentin's asking about you."

She threw me a skeptical look. I held her gaze—because blinking will give you away if you're lying. "He asked about me?"

"Oh yeah," I said.

"You're a terrible liar, Vic. Anyway, I have homework," Nevaeh said dismissively, writing in her notebook. I watched for another minute, but it didn't look like she was going to change her mind, so I went back downstairs.

"I've thought it over," I announced, even though Q didn't look up when I entered the room. "We need to keep this lean and mean, just the two of us. That way, there's less chance of getting discovered."

It didn't even seem like he'd heard me. Which should've been annoying, but I was actually starting to appreciate it. In a lot of ways, he was the perfect sidekick. Nice and quiet, and unless you tried to move him somewhere he didn't want to go, he pretty much did what he was told. I mean, when you're as cool as I am, you kind of need the opposite of that to balance you out, right? Once I reunited him with his mom, I'd be a little sorry to see him go.

"Obviously," I said, scooping two more Oreos off the plate, "first thing we need to do is find out where you live, right?"

"Six nineteen Maple Avenue," he said promptly.

I blinked at him, surprised. "Seriously, dude? I've been asking all day."

"Too much noise," he mumbled.

I wasn't sure what he meant, but hey, he'd just made my job a heck of a lot easier. "So, what part of town is that in?" Q looked confused, so I elaborated. "Hancock Park? Los Feliz? Beverly Hills? Oh man, is it Beverly Hills? Because that would be seriously awesome—"

"Torrance, California," he said. "Consistently ranked as one of the safest cities in Los Angeles County."

"Oh." I frowned. I wasn't totally sure where Torrance was, but if it was far away, buses might not go there. *Dang.* If I had access to my Ducati 900, we'd be all set, but I wasn't supposed to ride it anymore until I got an official license. Which was ridiculous, because I was seriously a natural at riding motorcycles. I could probably be a professional racer if I wanted, even though—

I realized Q had said something while I was distracted, picturing myself cornering a sweet Ducati at a racetrack. "What?"

"Mommy is not there," he said.

"Well, then where is she?"

"Hospital." His face kind of tensed up. "Mommy is sick."

"Oh." Well, that explained a lot. DCFS wouldn't place him in a home unless they knew he'd be there for a while, so it must be pretty bad. "What kind of sick?"

"Cancer," he said.

"Ah man." I shook my head. "Sorry, dude. Is she going to get better?"

He didn't answer, and suddenly I totally got it. The kid's mom was dying somewhere, and typically, DCFS was too busy to take him to visit her. All he wanted was to see his mom before she died, to hold her hand and tell her he loved her, and . . .

Q was staring at me. I realized my cheeks were wet and quickly wiped them dry. "Stupid allergies. All right, here's the plan. We get you to the hospital, right?"

Q got up from the chair and started heading for the door. I waved my hands to stop him and said, "Whoa, easy, dude. We can't go until the weekend." He didn't look convinced, so I explained, "Listen, if we don't show up at school, they'll call Mrs. K. And then Mrs. K will send us away, and we'll get split into different homes. You think the next kids are going to help you? 'Cause I can tell you right now, they won't." I got another flash of Mario, and added, "Trust me. Most people only look out for themselves. Me, I'm different."

Q still didn't look happy, but he said, "Saturday."

"Sure, Saturday." I clapped my hands together. "That gives us two full days to plan." Taking in his look of confusion, I waved it off. "Not you, dude. Don't worry. I got this."

## NEVAEH

Whatever Vic was up to with the new kid, he decided to keep it to himself after I missed their little "planning meeting." Which suited me just fine—I couldn't afford to waste time anyway. I had two quizzes on Friday and a paper due, and I needed to get As across the board to stay at the top of my class.

So I worked right up until it was time to make dinner. Mrs. K had called to say that she was sorry, but they wanted her to work a double, so she wouldn't be back until ten o'clock. So I made macaroni and cheese for the third time this week, which Vic grumbled about until I told him to shut it. Quentin and Mara just shoveled it in. A thank-you would've been nice, but at least they weren't complaining. After that, I washed the dishes, started the lunches for the next day, and ran the vacuum downstairs. I gave Mara her bath and tucked her in, then knocked on the boys' door.

"Lights-out in ten minutes! Those teeth better be brushed!"

Vic muttered something, and I heard what sounded like a shoe hitting the door. "A shower wouldn't hurt, either," I added, raising my voice. "You're seriously starting to smell, Vic."

"Not as bad as you!" he shouted back. Ignoring him, I scooped up the clothes from the bathroom hamper, started a load of laundry, then went back into our bedroom and clicked on the desk lamp.

A few minutes later, I felt eyes on my back and turned to discover Mara sitting up in bed, staring at me.

"What?" I asked.

She said something in Spanish. I looked around the room. "Oh, right. Hang on, I'll find him."

Mara had this nasty old clown doll that could inspire some serious nightmares, and she refused to go to sleep without it. Which wouldn't be a problem, except that every so often it completely vanished, and I had to search the entire house for it. I'd asked her repeatedly to keep track of it, but she'd just stare at me with those big brown eyes.

Honestly, sometimes it seemed like that clown got up and walked off on its own. It's that creepy.

Tonight I found it under the living room couch, along with assorted Oreo crumbs. I made a mental note to yell at Vic again about eating in the living room, then trudged back upstairs with the clown.

The shower was running, so Vic had actually listened to me for once. I handed Mara the doll, rubbed her back for a few minutes until she fell asleep, then practically crawled over to my desk chair.

I still had three more pages to write on the "power of fate" in *Holes*. I sighed and rubbed my eyes. Mara was snoring quietly behind me, and I could hear Vic murmuring through the wall. Quentin was dead silent as usual.

I tilted back in my chair and stared up at the ceiling, rubbing my neck. Out of nowhere my face suddenly got hot, and tears welled behind my eyes. It happened sometimes, this need to cry; fighting it only made it worse. When I was younger, there was always a specific reason: another foster kid hitting me or taking my stuff, getting bullied at school, that sort of thing. The worst was when I won the sixth-grade science fair. As I stood onstage with my trophy, I stared out at the sea of clapping parents in the audience and realized there was no one there for me, no one who even cared. Crying, I threw the trophy in a dumpster on the way home.

But lately, the tears came for no reason at all. Never in front of other people, of course; I had a handle on that. But maybe because I waited, the grief snuck up on me. In science there's something called a cascade reaction—like when you drop a Mentos into Diet

Coke. The bubbles in the soda are $CO_2$ that's basically looking for a way out, and when the Mentos dissolves to a certain point, it throws open a big doorway and *boom*! The $CO_2$ explodes.

So that's what happens with me. The little stuff just grows and grows until I can't hold it in anymore.

I pushed back from the desk so the tears wouldn't stain my essay and sobbed quietly so I wouldn't wake Mara. When I was done, I wiped my face dry and stared at the empty wall above my desk.

"A huge living room," I whispered. "Real wood floors, and nice rugs, the kind that feel like silk against your feet." It was a game I played when I got sad, picturing my perfect home. When I was younger, it was all pink lace and rainbows and a giant four-poster bed, based on something from a TV show.

Now that I was older, I wanted something else. "Floor-to-ceiling windows with a view," I continued. "Of a river, or maybe even the ocean. A doorman who only lets people in after checking if I want to see them. And a cat."

Tears threatened again—the cat did that to me sometimes. I'd had a puppy once for a couple of days, a stray I'd found in a box behind a dumpster on the way home from school. I snuck him into the house and stashed him in the closet, sneaking scraps from the kitchen to feed him. When my foster mom at the time found out, she totally freaked. She tore the puppy out of my arms and marched away with him. I never saw him again. I could still hear him whimper sometimes in my dreams.

Cats were safer, because they didn't need you as much. They were cleaner, too. "A short-haired one that won't shed on my white couch. Two bedrooms—"

Eyes closed, I constructed the entire future apartment in my head, room by room. I'd have it someday when I was a doctor. And no one would be able to take it away from me.


# QUENTIN

Loud Boy says the quest is on Saturday. I hope that we go before breakfast, since it is never *a well-balanced meal*, just cereal that turns the milk funny colors.

Tall Girl is not coming after all. Loud Boy says that we do not need her, although I suspect he might be mistaken, because she seems like *the reliable sort, steady as the day is long*, and Loud Boy is not. Still, he says we can get to Torrance without her.

It seems to be taking a long time for the quest to begin. But in *Star Wars: Episode IV* it took Luke a long time to leave Tatooine, and he had many adventures before he got to the Death Star, so maybe school is like Tatooine.

School is still loud, but sometimes the lady in the front of the room smiles at me, although she never offers me treats if I do something right. However, I have not answered any of her questions yet—maybe if I did, there would be treats.

It does not matter. On Saturday we will find Mommy, and I will be back in my own bed with my own dresser (four nicks on top, but *still has a lot of useful life in it*) and my own bedside table with the special edition R2-D2 alarm clock that goes *beep beep* when it is time to wake up (*precisely seven thirty, no lollygagging in bed all day!*).

I think of my clock and of Mommy, and tonight that does not make me cry because I will see her soon. I close my eyes and Mommy is there. She is smiling and I smile back and she says, *Welcome home, Quentin. Would you like a treat?*

# SIX

## VIC

I don't like to brag, but when it comes to planning an operation, I'm seriously awesome. I mean, man—just two days to pull this quest together, which is hardly any time at all; with the Brussels job, I had, like, weeks. But at the crack of dawn on Saturday, Q and me were geared up and ready for anything. Well, at least ready for Torrance.

Mrs. K works a double on Fridays, so she usually sleeps all day Saturday. You could probably march a herd of elephants past her bed and she wouldn't even roll over, that's how out of it she is. Still, I told Q to keep his shoes off as we went downstairs.

We each had a backpack. In mine was a full canteen (but really a water bottle), six energy bars, a length of rope (you never know when rope might come in handy—we might have to climb out of a third-story window, or onto a train or something), a Swiss army knife (from my dad, and it's seriously cool—it has scissors and everything), a pack of gum (chewing helps me concentrate, and boy, would I need that today!), and my bus pass.

I gave Q a water bottle and some snacks, too. He wouldn't let me touch his backpack; he was still sleeping with it, and didn't even take it off when he was sitting at his desk at school. I mean, you'd think he had nuclear codes in there or something, the way he treated that thing.

He seemed a lot happier, though. Once we got downstairs he went straight to the door and stood there staring at it, like a dog waiting for someone to come home. He kept turning around, as if making sure I was still coming.

"Give me a sec," I muttered, keeping my voice down. Nevaeh had missed her chance to come along, and I definitely didn't want her waking up and trying to stop us. I felt a little badly about it; it's not like she got many opportunities for adventure. But it was probably safer to keep this operation small.

I'd just finished tying my shoes and was slinging on my pack when I felt a tug on my elbow. Mara was standing there. It freaked me out how she did that, appearing out of nowhere like a ghost or something.

"Go back to bed!" I hissed.

She asked in Spanish where we were going. I told her it was none of her darn business—it was top secret, and she didn't have the security clearance.

Q was practically pawing at the door now. To be honest, I'd planned on eating a little breakfast, but it was clear that if we waited any longer, he might start freaking out again. I gave Mara a little shove toward the kitchen and said, "Go eat something. But be quiet; don't wake Mrs. K!"

"*¿Dónde vais?*" she asked again.

"Mommy," Quentin said. For a minute I was totally taken aback, like, *Does this guy speak Spanish and I just didn't know it?* But then I realized he was just reminding me we had to go.

"Mommy?" Mara repeated.

"That's right, I'm going to help Quentin find his mommy. But when Nevaeh wakes up, tell her we went to the library or something." I said it in Spanish, because it wasn't clear how much English she understood yet. She only spoke to us in Spanish, so my guess was not much.

She stared at us for another second, then shuffled toward the kitchen.

"Okay," I said, turning back to Q. "Let's blow this joint!"

# NEVAEH

The minute I woke up, I sensed that something was wrong. I groaned and checked the clock: six a.m. And I'd really been looking forward to sleeping in.

I checked the bottom bunk: Mara wasn't there, and her shoes were gone, too.

I swung my legs over and hopped down, careful to land softly. Less than a minute later, I was fully dressed. I crept down the hallway: the boys' room was empty. The feeling of foreboding grew as I tiptoed downstairs.

"Mara!" I said as loudly as I dared. "Vic!"

No answer. I checked the kitchen, dining room, living room, and backyard: no one. Standing back in the front hall, I realized that the front door was unbolted.

They were gone.

I yanked open the door and raced onto the porch, checking the sidewalk in both directions. The street was completely empty.

"Oh no," I said, realization dawning. Vic had taken Quentin to try to find his mother. For once, he was actually doing something instead of just acting it out in his head. But why had he taken Mara, too? It didn't make any sense.

My heart was hammering in my chest, and I could barely hear through the rush of blood in my ears. The chances of Vic getting them back safely ranged from remote to none. It was much more likely that we'd be getting a call from the hospital or the police station, and then Mrs. K would shunt us all back to the Welcome Center. I couldn't let that happen.

"Stupid, stupid, stupid," I muttered as I hurried back inside to grab my sneakers. My hands shook slightly as I tied them. The only thing Vic had to do was stay out of trouble; I handled everything else. And did he appreciate it? Did he thank me? No, he just kept finding ways to make my life harder. I was going to kill him.

But first I had to find him.

Thankfully, knowing Vic, he'd probably left a pretty clear trail. I tiptoed back upstairs to the boys' bedroom.

True to form, the desk was covered with scribbled-on papers. Most of them said stuff like, "Cut through wall with laser cannon!" and "Use base-jumping parachute to get back to street level!"

Halfway through the mess, though, I found a map he must've printed out in the computer lab at school. There was a red line leading directly from our house to . . .

"Torrance?" I said in disbelief, reading aloud. That was miles away! Had he completely lost his mind?

At the bottom of the page were directions for getting there on public transportation. It was a long, complicated list of steps, involving almost two and a half hours of switching from buses to trains and back, sometimes walking a few miles between stations. It was so much worse than I'd imagined.

I squeezed my eyes shut, already exhausted. I'd planned to spend the day finishing up my science fair project. Instead, I'd be chasing down my useless foster siblings.

*They couldn't have much of a head start*, I told myself. The first step on the map was taking the 92 bus downtown. That stop was a few blocks away, and at this hour on a Saturday, the buses wouldn't be running frequently. If I hurried, I might be able to catch up before they boarded one.

Determined, I grabbed my wallet and hurried back to the front door.

## QUENTIN

We are on a bus. Mommy and me never take buses, because they are *breeding grounds for germs*, but Loud Boy says this is the fastest way to get to Torrance, so I sit next to him and try very hard not to touch anything. I did not have a pass for the bus, but Loud Boy explained to the man that I had lost it, and the man did not look happy but he let us on.

We had only gone one block when the bus suddenly stopped and the quiet girl climbed on. This made Loud

Boy upset. He yelled at her in words I could not understand, but she did not say anything, instead she came and sat down next to us.

I like Quiet Girl because she is the quietest person I have ever met.

"Sheesh, she's still wearing pajamas!" Loud Boy says, sitting down again. "Nevaeh is going to kill me!" He gives her an angry look and says, "I should take you home right now!"

Quiet Girl does not say anything; she just stares at us. My heart is going *thump thump* because we are already on the bus and I do not want to go back to the house that is not home.

The girl says something to Loud Boy, and they talk for a minute, then he shakes his head and throws his hands up, nearly hitting me. "Okay, fine! Mara wants to help, dude. And she says if we take her back, she'll wake up Mrs. K and tell her everything."

Mrs. K is the one who looks sad all the time and does not seem to care that *a smile is a curve that sets a lot of things straight.* Mommy and me practice smiling in the mirror and she says that my smile makes her heart grow three sizes, just like the Grinch, who was also not very nice at first but became nicer. I do not want to go back and see Mrs. K; she does not seem like someone who will become nicer. Loud Boy must not want to, either, because he just sits there making angry noises and the bus keeps going and that is a relief.

The bus stops nine more times. Most of the houses are the same dirty brown color as the house that is not home, but there are also stores and other buildings. None of them are buildings I know; this is still not Torrance. Loud Boy jumps up and says, "C'mon!" and we both follow him off the bus (without touching anything!).

We are standing on a street and Loud Boy pulls a water bottle and a bar and a piece of paper out of his bag. He drinks the water and takes a bite of the bar and looks at the paper, then he says, "This way—it's a two-minute walk to the next bus." Quiet Girl and me follow him, and I am happy because we are on our way!

# SEVEN

## VIC

Well, it's going pretty darn well so far if I do say so myself. Except for Mara following us, which obviously wasn't part of the plan. Nevaeh is probably awake by now, totally freaking out. But there's not much I can do about it; when I threatened to take Mara back home, she said she'd rat us out. I kind of doubt she'd actually go through with it; I mean, she'd get in trouble, too. But like Commander Baxter always says, for a mission to succeed you need to adapt to changing circumstances, which is why I decided to keep going. If we stuck to the schedule, we'd be back by fifteen hundred, and Mrs. K wouldn't even know we'd been gone.

Since we'd skipped breakfast, I ate an energy bar to refuel while we walked to the 910 bus toward Inglewood. From there, we'd take the Metro Green Line, then transfer to another bus. After that it was just a three-mile walk to Torrance Memorial Medical Center.

Piece of cake. Mara was giving me a hungry look, so I handed her the last few bites of my bar. "Hey, man," I said to Q. "You hungry?"

He shook his head. I gotta say: when Q's got a goal, the kid's determined. I mean, he was sticking so close, he was practically tripping on my heels. If he knew the way to the bus stop, he'd probably be running there.

Mara looked ridiculous in her Dora pajamas: the cuffs were too long, since Mrs. K always made us buy a size up so that they'd last longer. Mara was working hard at not tripping, focusing on her feet the whole time, keeping that freaky clown doll buried up by her neck. Thank God she'd remembered to put on a pair of shoes, because there was a ton of broken glass on the ground. I thought about stopping to roll her cuffs, but we were on a tight schedule and really needed to catch that bus.

It said on my directions that it was a two-minute walk to Hill and First, but it turned out to be more like ten once you factored in waiting for traffic lights to change. I'd actually never been to this part of LA before; it was kind of weird, much more like a city than Echo Park, with lots of tall buildings. But there weren't any people around; it was like one of those zombie apocalypse movies, where the hero is in a huge city but it's really quiet. Thinking about that got me a little paranoid; I half expected to see a horde of the living dead come shuffling out of a construction site as we passed by. Honestly, I'd be glad when we got on the next bus. This place was seriously creeping me out.

At least there wasn't anyone around to ask what a bunch of kids were doing downtown at oh-six-thirty on a Saturday morning, including an eight-year-old girl wearing pajamas. Because that would be tough to explain.

We got lucky: a 910 bus pulled up right as we got to the intersection. I climbed on and waved my pass at the driver. I was about to launch into an explanation of why Quentin and Mara didn't have bus passes, but he just waved impatiently and said, "Move it, kids, I'm behind schedule!"

So obviously our luck was holding. I went to the back of the bus: we'd be on this one for a while, might as well get comfortable. It started moving before we got to our seats, and Quentin nearly fell on top of me; the kid refused to touch anything for some strange reason. Luckily, we were the only people on board. "Hold on to my backpack," I instructed, because that seemed to stress him out less than taking my shoulder.

We'd just gotten squared away when I heard a familiar voice yelling, "Hey!" outside the window. I swiveled in my seat and peered out: Nevaeh was chasing after the bus, her braids flying, waving her hands frantically to get the bus driver's attention.

I swallowed hard; she looked mad. I mean really, crazy mad. Especially when the bus driver chose to ignore her and instead gunned the engine, picking up speed as we drove deeper into the depths of downtown.

## NEVAEH

Oh boy, am I angry. I swear I might actually strangle Vic when I catch up to him. He looked right at me out that bus window, but did he tell the driver to stop? Nope. Instead, he left me standing there panting as the bus turned a corner and sped off.

I had a stitch in my side and was covered in sweat. I'd never been in this part of downtown before—it was nasty, all boarded-up buildings and gutters clogged with trash. The whole place smelled like pee, too—not exactly what I was in the mood for this early on a Saturday morning.

I stalked to the nearest bus stop and checked the route map, then compared it to the printout from Vic's desk. According to his directions, they were taking that bus all the way to a subway station across town. I could get on the next bus and hope to catch up to them, but it was kind of a long shot. I chewed my lip, trying to come up with another option.

I ran my finger down the list of connections. There

it was: a few blocks away, another bus ran parallel to the 910. With any luck, it would make fewer stops, and I'd manage to intercept them before they reached the subway station.

And then I'd drag Vic home by the hair if I had to.

## QUENTIN

Quiet Girl will not stop staring at me. She sits in the seat across the aisle and chews on her hair and looks at me. I like her pajamas; they have Dora on them. I used to watch Dora with Mommy, it was my favorite next to the Star Wars movies, which of course are the best because they have actual science! But in *Dora the Explorer*, there was a backpack and a map and a monkey named Boots and they have adventures with *educational value*. Dora the Explorer says that "*azul*" is blue and "*amarillo*" is yellow and "*rojo*" is red. And counting is *uno, dos, tres* . . .

Loud Boy says, "Are you counting?"

He is giving me a funny look. I point to the pajamas. "Dora."

"Yeah, right, man. That's Dora."

"*La Exploradora*," Quiet Girl says. She smiles at me.

"You like that show?" Loud Boy asks.

I do not say anything. Mommy always says *needless chatter clouds the mind*. I remember Mommy sitting on the couch patting the safe spot on my head while we watched Dora and the monkey help a train win a race.

"Hey, dude. No crying," Loud Boy says.

Quiet Girl does not say anything, but she reaches across the aisle and touches my hand and says, "*Me gusta Dora también.*"

I usually do not like it when people touch me, but her hand just feels like air, so I say, "Swiper no swiping," and Quiet Girl laughs and then Loud Boy laughs too. They are laughing so hard it makes me forget to be sad and then the bus is stopping and Loud Boy says, "Right on schedule!" and we get off again.

# EIGHT

## VIC

"Okay, we walk from here," I said after consulting the map. It wasn't even oh-seven-hundred yet, and we were nearly halfway to Torrance; not bad, especially considering I was the only one who'd brought my bus pass. I was a little worried about switching to a train; bus drivers were usually pretty chill, they could care less if kids got on so long as they didn't make any trouble. But I didn't know much about the subway; I'd only taken it once, for a school trip to a free concert. The music was kind of lame, but it was in this amazing symphony hall that looked like a spaceship and was built by Walt Disney, so how cool is that?

Mario had sat next to me at the concert, even though he was three years older, and they let him because everyone thought he was my brother for real. He'd snuck in some Red Vines; I don't know where he got them, but Mario always had a stash of candy and he was super cool about sharing. I wondered if he still did that. Maybe there was another kid somewhere who slept on the top bunk, and got to share Mario's candy and laugh at his awesome jokes. He had this great one about penguins that was completely hilarious; every time he told it I'd laugh so hard I nearly choked—

I realized that Mara and Q were just standing there staring at me. We were still a few blocks from the train station. To be honest, I wasn't totally sure which way to go. I didn't have my company-issued GPS system because obviously that's not the kind of equipment they just let you take home, and it wasn't so easy to find things without it.

"Hang on," I said. "I'm just trying to figure out which way is north."

Mara pointed back in the direction we'd come from and said, "*Norte.*" I was about to snap that she couldn't possibly know that, but then I realized she was right. "I knew that," I muttered.

She didn't say anything, and neither did Q; they just kept looking at me like, *Why aren't we moving yet?* So I started walking east toward the subway station.

After a couple of blocks I realized that I might, accidentally, have confused east with west. That happens sometimes, even to a seriously talented spy like me; I mean, a lot of people get their left hand confused with their right, right?

Anyway, nothing around us looked like a metro station; instead, we were under an overpass. There were cardboard boxes everywhere, and lots of trash. Way overhead, a whole bunch of highways crisscrossed each other like twisted ribbons. They actually kind of reminded me of that crazy symphony hall.

Q looked around and said, "This is not Torrance."

"Man, you're turning into a regular chatterbox," I muttered. Out of nowhere, he'd started counting in Spanish on the bus, and now this. I kind of preferred him not talking, to be honest.

"We're lost," Mara said in Spanish. It had never occurred to me before, but she actually kind of looked like Dora, with her big eyes and bowl cut. Except the real Dora would be a lot more helpful in this situation. At least she could read a map.

"We're not lost," I retorted. "I was just . . . testing, to see if either of you were paying attention. And guess what? You failed."

Neither of them looked very impressed. "Anyway, c'mon." I shrugged my pack higher on my shoulders and turned back the way we'd come. "It's this way."

We'd only gone ten feet when I heard something growling. And when I say "growling," I mean it sounded like a lawn mower starting up, but a heck of a lot scarier. One thing about me that you might not know is that I don't like dogs. I mean, I know there are crazy-cool K-9 dogs that are real cops and soldiers. But when I was younger, we had a neighbor who used to train dogs to fight, and one of them got into our yard once, and . . . well, let's just say it was bad.

So I stopped dead, thinking, *Please be a Chihuahua, please be a Chihuahua* . . . But it's never a Chihuahua when you want it to be, right? Instead, this huge pit bull came out from behind the stack of boxes in front of us. Its head was low, ducked beneath massive shoulders. The dog's teeth were bared, and it was walking real slow, like a lion on a nature show.

And suddenly, I couldn't move. I mean, all my elite training went right out the window. I wanted to run, I was telling my feet to run, but I couldn't seem to get them to listen. Instead I just stared at this dog and started praying as it came closer and closer. Drool dripped from its fangs as it snarled even louder. Then it broke into angry barking and lunged for us.

## NEVAEH

I got lucky and caught the other bus right as it was pulling up; I had to run, but this driver wasn't a total jerk, so he waited for me.

I sat in the front, silently willing it to move faster as we lumbered south. I could picture the other bus moving parallel to us a few blocks away. At this hour on a Saturday, there weren't many other passengers, so at most of the stops the driver just slowed down, then shifted back into gear when it was clear that no one was getting off or on.

I fervently hoped that Vic's bus was stopping at every stop, and that maybe someone was loading on a bike or something, too; anything to slow them down.

I got off at the bus stop closest to the metro station and ran the final three blocks. I had to use three dollars' worth of grocery money to buy a metro card, which did nothing to improve my mood. I slid it through the scanner and pushed past the turnstile, then took the stairs to the platform two at a time.

There were only a few people waiting for a train, and none of them were my irritating foster siblings. According to the computerized sign overhead, the next Green Line train wasn't due for twelve minutes, which was a bad sign. If a train had just left, and they'd managed to catch it, they were already headed to Inglewood. Going all the way there to track them down would take at least another hour.

"I am seriously going to kill Vic," I muttered.

An older white guy waiting on the platform gave me a funny look. He didn't look like a creep, so I decided it was probably safe to talk to him.

"Excuse me," I said loudly. "Did you see three kids come through here?"

He shook his head. "Nope. Sorry, miss."

"Okay. Did I just miss a train?"

"Not sure. Just got here a minute ago myself," he said with a shrug, then turned back to his paper.

I pulled out the copy of Vic's map again and glared at it. *Where are they?* Was he following a different route after all? Maybe Vic had left this copy behind because he'd come up with a better way to get to Torrance. If that was true, this might all be a wasted trip. Maybe I should just go home and come clean to Mrs. K.

The thought made my stomach hurt. I could practically hear her mumbling about how tired she was, and how maybe she was no good at being a foster mother anymore. Then Ms. Judy from DCFS would show up, and I'd probably be back at the Welcome Center by dinner.

I dropped onto a bench and put my head in my hands. It didn't seem to matter what I did, or how hard I tried. My life always fell apart anyway. I hated the thought of starting over again in a new foster home. Leaving the few friends I'd managed to make, like Jada. Dealing with new teachers and a new locker code, and getting lost in the halls because I didn't know where anything was . . .

I smacked my head, suddenly realizing what had probably happened. Vic had a terrible sense of direction; he still had trouble finding his way home from school—that's why I always had to walk him. It would be just like him to go the wrong way. If I checked the blocks around the train station, I'd probably find him standing there like an idiot.

I sprang off the bench and ran back to the stairs. I did a quick circle around the station, but didn't see them. *Of course*, I thought. *That would be way too easy.* I'd have to be methodical about it, circling the station one block at a time. That way, I'd be less likely to miss them.

Nothing for the first few blocks. My spirits started to flag again; maybe they *had* caught a train before I got there.

Then, a few blocks west of the train station, I stepped beneath an overpass and saw the three of them standing there. I heaved a sigh of relief, then marched toward them, calling out, "Vic Quintero, you are in so much—"

I froze, suddenly spotting what they were all staring at. Between us was the biggest pit bull I'd ever seen. It was covered in battle scars, snarling and barking ferociously as it paced back and forth in front of them. Vic was staring at it, shaking slightly. Mara and Quentin were huddled behind him.

I'd heard some pretty terrible things about pit bulls. I'd been in a foster home once with a kid who'd been attacked by one, and he still walked with a cane. He said that once they got their jaws around something, they clamped down so hard it was impossible to make them let go. They could rip out your throat without even trying very hard. They could kill you in under a minute.

Even though I was mad at Vic, I couldn't let anything happen to him.

"Hey!" I yelled, waving my arms in the air above my head like a lunatic.

The dog turned to look at me. I searched the ground for something to throw, hoping to chase it away, but there was nothing but cardboard and trash. I took a step forward. My mouth dried up as the dog growled louder. I didn't know what to do; my whole body was screaming at me to run. Vic stood there with his mouth hanging open. He looked completely terrified.

The dog swung its head back and forth between us, like it couldn't decide who to attack first. It was breathing hard—was that foam on the corner of its mouth? Did it have rabies? People died from that, didn't they?

*I have to get it away from them*, I kept thinking, over and over.

The dog stepped toward me, its head lolling to the

side. He stared at me, as if trying to figure out how I was going to taste. I was so focused on it, I didn't see Mara until it was too late.

Somehow she'd gotten around Vic and was standing right behind the dog, less than a foot away from it. And she was holding something in her hand.

"Mara!" I yelled. "Get back!"

Mara acted like she hadn't heard me. She was totally focused on the dog. Its head whipped around to confront this new threat.

Vic was yelling at her too. Everything seemed to slow down as Mara slowly extended her hand toward the dog. She was whispering to it in Spanish. I ran toward her, toward it, but I was too far away, I wasn't going to get there in time—

"Stop!" A hand clamped down on my arm, jerking me back.

Instinctively, I yanked free and whirled toward the voice. A filthy homeless guy with matted hair was standing there. He smelled terrible. He held both hands out toward me and started babbling. "Easy, now. Gus is a good boy. He won't hurt your friend; he's just a little protective of my camp is all. . . ."

I heard a giggle, and turned to see Mara feeding the dog something from her hand. Its hackles had gone down, and it made slurping noises as it chewed noisily, practically smacking its lips.

"That's your dog?" I demanded. My hands were shaking, and my knees felt like they might give out.

"Yes, miss." His head bobbed. "Sorry for the trouble. Gus is all bark, you see—"

"Mara, come over here!"

Obediently, Mara walked toward me. The dog trotted after her, panting happily. He looked completely different now, almost like a puppy.

"You sure do have a way with him, little girl," the homeless guy said appreciatively. "Gus doesn't take to just anyone, y'know."

The cuffs of Mara's pajamas were filthy, and her chin was streaked with chocolate. I grabbed her hand. "Vic! Quentin! Get over here right now!"

"You kids out here all alone?" the homeless guy asked.

"No. Our parents are right over there," I said, pointing back toward the metro station.

"Your parents?" he asked skeptically, taking us in.

"Foster parents," I amended, making sure the kids stayed behind me as I backed away from him. "And we're not supposed to talk to strangers."

"Well, now, that's a good policy." The homeless man's head was still bobbing—I wondered if something was wrong with him. "Sure is, sure is. You should be careful, though. Not so safe around here for kids."

"We're going," I said curtly. Vic was still white as

a sheet, all his usual bluster gone. Quentin looked the same as always; I wondered if he'd even realized they were in danger.

"I—I don't feel so good," Vic mumbled.

"It would've served you right if you'd gotten bit!" I snapped. "Now come on, we're going home."

"You take care of those little ones, now," the man said.

I didn't answer. I was marching away when Mara suddenly broke free of my grip and ran back toward him. "Mara, stop!" I yelled.

When she was a foot away, she held out her hand, the same way she had with the dog, and handed the homeless guy a wrapped energy bar. He broke into a wide grin that showed yellow, broken teeth. "Thank you, miss. Much appreciated."

Mara smiled, then ran back to me. I didn't have the heart to chastise her. Squaring my shoulders, I led them back toward the bus stop.

# QUENTIN

I do not understand what is happening. Loud Boy said we were right on schedule, and I was thinking how pleased Mommy would be because she thought it was important to stick to a schedule—*routine is our friend*—and then we were in a dark, smelly place filled with boxes and there was a giant dog that looked like it wanted to bite us, but it did not because Quiet Girl made friends with it. And Tall Girl is here now even though Loud Boy said she is not part of the plan, and we are walking back the way we came and that does not seem right so I stop. Loud Boy stops too. His face is frowning and his hair is all messed up.

Tall Girl and Quiet Girl stop, too, and Tall Girl says, "Hurry up, I don't have all day!" She sounds angry, and I decide that maybe she is not so nice after all.

Loud Boy says, "We're not going back."

And Tall Girl says, "Oh yes, you are. This is not up for discussion." She sounds like a mommy even though she is not a mommy and that is confusing.

"We're not done with the quest."

"There is no quest!" Tall Girl yells so loud I cover my ears.

"We're halfway there!" Loud Boy yells back.

I hate all the yelling. Mommy and me never yelled, except for one time when I touched the stove and it was hot, hot, hot.

"I don't care!" Tall Girl yells. Quiet Girl is now covering her ears too. We look at each other, and I can tell she does not like the yelling, either.

"Well, you can't make us." Loud Boy starts to walk away from us.

"You're going the wrong way again, you idiot!

There's no way you'll get to Torrance when you can't even find the train station!"

"I can too!" he yells back. "Come on, Q."

I start to follow Loud Boy, because he said he would take me to Mommy. Although I am a little worried since he is walking back toward the angry dog.

"I'll tell Mrs. K."

"That'll just get you in trouble," Loud Boy says. "I'll tell her it was all your idea!"

"What?" Tall Girl looks even madder when he says this. "You wouldn't."

"Yeah, I would. So go ahead and take Mara. But we're not coming with you."

He keeps walking. Tall Girl makes an angry noise and runs after him. She grabs his arm to stop him and says something to him in a low voice. I cannot hear what she is saying, but he pulls his arm away and backs up.

These kids are very tiring, they are making me tired. When I felt like this, Mommy would put me down for a little nap so that I would wake up refreshed and *ready to tackle the day*. I wish I could take a nap now, but I do not want to sleep in a cardboard box like the smelly man—I think that maybe it is the boxes that make him smell so bad.

The two of them yell at each other while Quiet Girl and me wait. Finally, Tall Girl throws her arms up and says, "Fine!" and then comes back over and says, "After you see your mom, we're going straight home. Got it?"

I know that Mommy will make sure I never go back to the house that is not home, so I say, "Home." Tall Girl stands there for another minute, then she says, "Okay. The train station is this way. From now on, I'm in charge."

# NINE

## VIC

I've never been so angry before. I'm even madder than that time when a Russian spy tried to torture
secret codes out of me. I'm seriously tempted to just
turn around and head home. Forget Q, forget the quest,
forget everything.

But a true hero never gives up on a quest, not even
when he encounters mad dogs or confusing maps. And
we'd already overcome so much, from here on out it
was guaranteed to be smooth sailing. That's how it
always works in movies and books. I just had to keep
Nevaeh from dragging us back to the house.

So I threatened to tell on her (even though I never
would've; when I take a blood oath, I mean it. There are
literally dozens of secrets I'll take to the grave). Instead
of looking scared, though, Nevaeh leaned down and
said in a nasty voice, "Like you did with Mario?"

I asked, "What are you talking about?" because I honestly had no clue; she'd never met Mario. I wasn't even sure how she knew his name.

Nevaeh said, "When I moved in, Mrs. K said you were her eyes and ears. You told her some kid named Mario was stealing candy, and that got him sent away. She said you'd report back to her if I did anything wrong."

"No," I told her, shocked. "That's not what happened—"

"Bull." Nevaeh leaned in closer and hissed, "If you *ever* do that to me, I will make you pay for it. Understood?"

I stared at her. My stomach was churning, I still wasn't feeling very well; facing down that rabid dog really took it out of me. Maybe because of that, everything felt a little weird, like I was walking through a dream instead of real life.

All this time, had Nevaeh really thought that I was spying on her? I mean, it was a little hilarious, because what a serious waste of my talents that would've been, right? I straightened my shoulders and said, "Just so you know, if we don't complete this quest today, I'll just try again next weekend. You can't stop us."

Nevaeh glared at me, but I didn't back down. I was still really mad about what she'd said. Pretty angry with Mrs. K, too, for spreading lies about me; maybe it was time to tell Commander Baxter that I was ready to live in the DEEC dormitory after all.

"Mommy," Quentin called out. He and Mara were still standing ten feet away watching us. Mara was chewing on another bar, she had chocolate smeared all over her face. *That's it, no more energy bars for her*, I thought.

Nevaeh stared at them for a minute, then sighed and looked at her watch. "Well, today is ruined anyway. We're halfway there already, maybe once he talks to his mom, Quentin will stop freaking out. Then all this nonsense is over for good, you hear me? No more sneaking off, ever."

I nodded, and that's when Nevaeh basically took over. She led us three blocks to the subway. (Which I totally could've done; I mean, I'd already figured out the right way to go before she got there.) Then she added money to a metro card and used it to slide us all through the turnstile, grumbling the whole time about wasting grocery money on something so useless.

Look, I appreciated that she wasn't trying to make us go home anymore, but now she acted like she was in charge? She didn't want to be part of the quest to begin with! She didn't even come to the planning meeting! I was the one who'd spent hours (well, okay, maybe a half hour) in the school library figuring out which buses and trains to take, I was the one who'd remembered to pack provisions (and I can't believe Mara gave away all those energy bars instead of eating them—I mean, it was nice and all, but what if something happened, like an earthquake or a zombie apocalypse? We were already basically out of food, and we were only half-way there!).

I stood there on the subway platform, fuming while Nevaeh made a big show of double-checking my directions against the big map.

"I don't think there's a faster way to get there," she announced, and I was all like, *Yeah, I know—if there was, we'd already be doing it!* But I didn't say anything because I knew she'd just start yelling again, and I was too tired to keep fighting with her. I must not have slept very well, because suddenly all I wanted to do was shut my eyes.

We stood on the platform for a couple of minutes before a train showed up. Nevaeh hustled us on, and I took a seat a few rows behind her, just to be annoying. Her nostrils flared, so I could tell it had worked, but she just pulled out a tissue and started wiping Mara's face with it. The train lurched forward, and we headed toward Inglewood.

While I sat there staring out the train window, I couldn't stop thinking about what she'd said about Mario. She was totally wrong; I wanted to tell her that, but she probably wouldn't believe me. Mario had been my best friend. The only friend I'd ever had, really. I'd never meant to get him in trouble.

Here's what *really* happened: Usually when we went to the dentist, my teeth were totally perfect, because of my superior DNA. But last year, I ended up with two cavities. I told Ms. Judy afterward that it was probably because of all the candy Mario and I were eating. I didn't think it was a big deal, I was just having a conversation! And then Ms. Judy asked if Mrs. K gave us lots of candy, and I didn't want Mrs. K to get in trouble, so I told her the truth, that Mario had given it to me. When she asked where Mario got it, I told her I didn't know. And then she got real quiet, and didn't say anything else.

Then Ms. Judy had a "private conversation" with Mrs. K, and they both went up to our room and searched it. They found candy and other stuff like fancy pens and a watch and even an iPod touch. And that same night they took Mario away, and I never even got to say goodbye to him.

What Nevaeh said made me realize something horrible: maybe Mario thought I'd ratted him out on purpose. What if I'd never heard from him again because he was mad at me?

"Two more stops," Nevaeh said in her annoying fake grown-up voice.

I muttered a Spanish swear at her under my breath,

and she snapped, "I know what that means, you know."

I slumped down in the seat and closed my eyes. If Nevaeh wanted to be in charge, fine. She'd see how hard it was to stay on mission. Meanwhile, I could take a nap.

## NEVAEH

Okay, maybe I shouldn't have said that to Vic. But I was mad at him for dragging us here and putting Mara and Quentin in danger. My hands were still a little shaky, and I could hear the dog's growls in the back of my mind. That whole situation could have gotten really bad, really fast. I pictured an ambulance, sirens wailing. Mrs. K showing up at the hospital and telling me I'd let her down, and that she couldn't handle all this stress at her age, and we'd be better off in a different home . . .

Still, when I'd told Vic what she'd said about Mario, he'd looked like I'd slapped him. It was the main reason I'd always been so careful around him; I mean, he was always pretending to be a spy, right? It would make sense if he actually was one in real life.

But the look of hurt on his face gnawed at me. He and Quentin were a few rows behind us on the train. Quentin sat bolt upright, like a doll on a metal rod. Vic was slumped so low it looked like he'd slide off the seat and onto the floor at any moment.

I felt a twinge of guilt; Vic was only trying to help Quentin, after all. In his own, messed-up way, but still—not many other kids would bother.

I pulled myself up and staggered back to them, fighting the movement of the train. Stopping in the aisle, I said, "I won't tell Mrs. K about today."

Vic didn't even open his eyes. He looked awful.

"What's up with you?" I asked.

"Nothing," he said.

"Well, it would serve you right if you were getting sick," I snapped reflexively. Inwardly, I cursed myself; why was it so hard for me to be nice to him?

Quentin was watching me placidly. "Unfriendly dog," he offered.

"Yeah, and we got lucky," I said.

"Just go away," Vic mumbled.

"Fine. I'll tell you when we're getting off." Squaring my shoulders, I stalked back to Mara. She was still gnawing on an energy bar; the kids seemed to have brought an endless supply of them, for which I was secretly relieved. None of them were easy to handle when they got hungry. Her face was smeared with chocolate again, and she'd managed to get a lot of it on her clown doll, too. I went to wipe her face, then decided to wait—might as well save my tissues for our return trip.

I checked my watch: according to Vic's printout,

in ten more minutes we'd arrive at the Nash/Mariposa Station near Inglewood.

I'd stayed at a foster home in Inglewood for two months—that was where I'd found the puppy, actually. I felt a little tremor of hope; what if we got off the train and found him waiting on the platform for us, tail wagging, tongue lolling out the side of his mouth? I knew it was ridiculous, but I was still a little disappointed when we climbed off and there was no one there but a couple of rough-looking teenagers. I didn't like the look of them; their eyes were glassy like they were on something.

As I ushered Vic, Mara, and Quentin toward the exit, I kept my head down, avoiding eye contact. One of them said something, and the others laughed harshly. I stepped up the pace, hustling everyone toward the stairs. Vic lagged behind until I gave him a little shove and said, "Come *on*!"

"I'm coming!" he said dully.

I snuck a quick glance back over my shoulder; the teens weren't following us.

Relieved, I said, "Okay. We need to walk to the bus stop. The two-thirty-two should take us to Redondo Beach."

"I already knew that," Vic muttered.

I was seriously sick of his attitude, but arguing with him would only delay us. I took Mara's hand and made sure Quentin followed. Vic shuffled along behind us, scuffing his sneakers along the concrete. The rasping noise they made was beyond irritating, but I tried not to let it get to me. If Vic's schedule was right, we'd get to Torrance in another hour; after this final bus, we'd have to walk nearly three miles, which wasn't going to be fun. But we should get there by ten a.m. at the latest. If we managed to find his mom, Quentin could see her (and if we couldn't, too bad—as far as I was concerned, this "quest" was done as soon as we reached the hospital). We'd give it a shot, then we'd turn back. If we got home by early afternoon, I'd still have time to work on my science project. And I'd tell Mrs. K that we'd spent the day at the library. . . .

I sighed. Vic didn't understand how hard it was to be the responsible one all the time, the person everyone relied on. I'd give almost anything to be able to say, *Forget it, I'm doing what I want for a change.* But life didn't work like that. At least, mine didn't.

## QUENTIN

Mommy will be so surprised when I tell her that I like buses. I am not even worried about touching things anymore. I am just happy that we did not go back to the house that is not home after Tall Girl showed up. I am also happy that the giant dog did not eat Quiet

Girl, because that would have been sad. And her pajamas made me realize that we are on an adventure just
like Dora, and we even have a map. Dora takes buses
and trains like we do, and she does not worry about
getting sick, so maybe I should not worry, either.

A bus rocks back and forth, and it feels nice. And
no one is talking, so it is nice and quiet.

I also like trains; the train is quiet too, and it seems
very efficient. There are many signs inside that tell you
how to lose weight and who to call if you have been in
an accident, and all of that seems very helpful. I think
Mommy would be happy to know that trains can be
helpful and that there is a lot of information there that
people need.

I will take Mommy on a bus and a train, to show
her that it is not so bad. She can bring the special
spray for our hands to take care of the germs and then
we will not have to worry so much about touching
things.

I think Mommy will like the bus, and then we can
take it everywhere and see things like the Aquarium of
the Pacific, where there is a *New Sea Jellies Exhibit:
Open 9 a.m. to 6 p.m. Every Day of the Year Except
Christmas!* The sign on the train had a picture of a
jellyfish and two kids pointing at it with big smiles.
Jellyfish are nice and quiet, and maybe we can take one

home with us and I can keep it in a bowl next to my R2-D2 clock.

Vic does not seem to be enjoying the bus ride, he keeps bumping into me and his eyes are closed and he is still white—so white. He is not talking, either, even though he is always talking. I think about telling Tall Girl that Vic is not talking, but she does not look like she wants to talk, either, so instead I read the helpful signs that are also on the bus (*If you or someone you know has mesothelioma, call 1-888-Sue-Fast; Cash for Gold! Three locations, open daily, turn your old jewelry into coin!; Need to lose weight fast? Try Shred Fat!* Sue Fast and Shred Fat are close to the same, I think).

Quiet Girl is looking at me. I show her the signs and whisper, "Shred Fat and Sue Fast!" and she giggles. I like Quiet Girl. Maybe she could come live with me and Mommy and the jellyfish, and then she would smile more.

# TEN

## VIC

Wow, Redondo Beach is fancy. When we got off the bus, we all just stood there staring. I mean, we've got shops in Echo Park, sure, but nothing like this. There's a place called the Kool Dog Kafé that seriously seemed to be a coffee shop for dogs. Next to it was a fancy-looking restaurant called Buca di Beppo, and next to that was a hotel, the Riviera, which according to the sign had a sauna *and* a fitness club. Right in front of us was an office with a giant plate-glass window that read, *Tom Duluth Public Relations*, and inside it looked like the living room from a TV show or something.

"What are public relations?" I asked Nevaeh.

"Probably something like introducing people to one another," Nevaeh said. Even though she was trying to hide it, I could tell she was impressed too.

Mara pointed up, and we all looked. There were seagulls flying past overhead. I mean real, honest-to-God seagulls.

"*La playa*," Mara said in a sad little voice.

I looked back at my map, which was pretty crinkled and had some chocolate stains on it. "She's right! The beach is only a few blocks away!"

"We're not going to the beach," Nevaeh said firmly, a total buzzkill as always.

"But—"

"No!" Nevaeh said, jutting out her lower lip. I considered arguing with her; I mean, even Quentin kind of perked up when I said "beach," so I bet he'd never been, either. I pictured us all taking off our shoes and running across the sand to the water. Splashing one another and maybe even building a sandcastle. But Nevaeh was already walking away. And to be honest, even though I took a quick nap on the bus, I still wasn't feeling great. Maybe eating energy bars for breakfast wasn't the best idea.

Still, I had to tough it out. A really great spy didn't let something dumb like getting sick stop him from completing his mission. And it was my job to keep everyone calm, cool, and collected. I took a few sips of water from my canteen, which helped a little. Nevaeh might not realize it, but she needed my help. And even though she'd been seriously uncool, I wouldn't let that get in the way of doing the right thing.

We rounded the corner, and I nearly crashed straight into Nevaeh. She'd stopped dead because the street was blocked off. A huge sign overhead read, *Riviera Village Street Fair*, and there were a ton of people milling around all sorts of booths. It was loud and crowded, and I could practically feel Q tense up; I was getting pretty good at reading him, and he definitely didn't like crowds.

"Okay," Nevaeh said, sounding irritated. She squinted at the map. "If we go up two streets, then take a left, that should get us around it."

I looked at the street fair. The stands were bright and colorful, and all the people looked happy as they checked out necklaces and T-shirts and all sorts of food; the smell of churros and sausages and roasted nuts was overpowering. Maybe eating something besides energy bars would help me feel better. "There's grocery money left, right?" I said hopefully. "Maybe we could just—"

"We're not going in there," Nevaeh snapped. "Now come on, let's— Where's Mara?"

I looked around. Mara was gone. Nevaeh had let go of her hand to check the map, and she'd vanished; there was nothing but air where she'd just been.

"It's seriously spooky how she does that," I muttered, although of course I could do the same thing if I wanted to. I scanned the crowd for a pair of pink pajamas topped by dark black hair, but there were too many people moving around.

Nevaeh swore loudly and threw up her hands. "Seriously, do any of you ever listen to me?"

I was going to say that maybe people would listen more if she said things nicely, but I realized Q was pointing down the street. "I think he's saying she went that way."

"What?" Nevaeh whirled on Q. "Quentin, did you see where she went?"

"Dora," he said, still pointing toward the small Ferris wheel at the end of the street.

Nevaeh blew out her breath hard and said, "Great. Just great. I guess we're going in after all."

## NEVAEH

I was seriously at my wits' end. I mean, I let Mara out of my sight for five seconds—five seconds!—and she disappeared. Of all of them, Mara was the one I could usually count on. She silently did exactly what she was told, even when I wasn't entirely sure she'd understood me.

But then, before today I never would've expected her to follow Vic and Quentin, so maybe I didn't really know her at all. Maybe she was sick of always being the good one, too, so she'd decided that starting today, she was going to do whatever the heck she wanted, even if it messed things up for everyone else.

I tried not to think about all the bad things that could happen to a lost little girl in a strange place; Mara barely spoke English, so even if she wanted help, she probably couldn't ask for it. I didn't even know if she'd be able to tell people where our house was.

*Don't panic,* I reminded myself. *She's fine. She just got distracted and wandered off.*

"Stay close," I ordered the boys, who were both standing there like idiots gaping at the scene. "I mean it. No one goes more than a foot away from me. Is that clear?"

I needn't have bothered; as soon as we crossed the police barricade, they were practically walking on my heels. I was tempted to snap at them again, but they were just doing what I'd asked, so I gritted my teeth and pressed ahead.

Under other circumstances, this might actually have been fun. Not that we could afford anything; after buying the metro pass, I only had a couple of dollars left from the grocery money. And that definitely wasn't cash we could waste on something useless, like a necklace or T-shirt. As it was, we'd be eating a lot of mac and cheese again next week.

Still, the booths were tempting. There was one for face painting; I poked my head inside, but no Mara, just another girl around the same age getting a butterfly on her cheek. The next booth sold the type of cute T-shirts that Aliyah was always wearing. Another stall had tables full of ugly rocks that were cracked open to show colorful gems that looked like rock candy.

"Geodes," Vic said. "Man, those are cool. I've always wanted—"

"Keep looking for Mara," I reminded him sharply.

He glowered at me. I ignored him and kept pushing forward. It was getting more crowded, forcing us to slow to a shuffle. I fought the urge to scream.

"Mrs. K is going to be really mad that we lost her," Vic said.

"And whose fault is that?" I snarled, still scanning the crowd on both sides.

"Hey, I didn't want her to come," Vic whined. "She followed us."

"You should've taken her back right away."

"Then you would've stopped us," he said.

"Darn right I would've," I muttered.

"And then we wouldn't have been able to complete the quest."

I stopped and rubbed my eyes. A headache was forming at my temples. I was hot and thirsty and tired, saddled with two useless boys, miles from home, looking for a lost little girl. "There is no quest, Vic."

"There is," he insisted. "I promised Q—"

"So what?" I said, whipping around. I waved toward Quentin. "You think we'll find his mom at the hospital, and suddenly everything will be all right?"

"Well, yeah—"

"It won't!" I leaned forward until our faces were almost touching. "I'll tell you what's going to happen. If we find her, which is doubtful, she might be too sick to even recognize him. And that might make Quentin even worse. Did you ever think of that? There might be a reason why they won't let him see her!"

Vic stared back at me. A tear slipped down his right cheek. "But we have to try—"

"Why? Why do we have to try?" I gripped his shoulders and shook him slightly. "Don't you get it? We're on our own, all of us. No one wants us; if they did, we'd be with them."

"My dad—"

"Your dad isn't some top secret spy, Vic." I knew I should've stopped there, but I couldn't seem to help myself, the words tumbled out in a flood of frustration and anger. "I saw your file once when Mrs. K left it out. Your dad got deported. They caught him at a job site during an immigration sweep."

"You're lying. He's a freedom fighter." Vic's chin was trembling. For some reason, that made me even angrier.

"God, Vic, wake up! Your dad didn't *want* to go back to El Salvador; they *made* him. You should actually be happy he didn't abandon you. Maybe he'll even come back someday!" I leaned in. "And at least he's alive. My mother's dead, and I don't even know who my father was. You think I wouldn't like to pretend that they're both great people, doing something awesome? I would! But it wouldn't change anything!"

Tears flowed freely down his face now. "My dad wouldn't leave me behind. He would've come back for me."

I realized I was squeezing his shoulders too hard, and let go. "Maybe he thinks you're better off here," I said in a low voice. The expression on his face was awful: anguished and hurt. I bit my lip, then added more gently, "You can't live in a fantasy forever, Vic."

He looked terrible—tears and snot streamed down his face, and he was shaking. I should've just kept my mouth shut. What was wrong with me?

*Maybe you're not a very nice person*, said a small voice in my head. Right now, I certainly didn't feel like one. Vic wasn't hurting anyone with his imaginary spy stuff, and if it helped him cope, then who was I to burst his bubble? I had no idea why his dad hadn't come back, or why he'd ended up in foster care instead of with relatives—his file didn't explain that.

Our files usually left a lot of important stuff out.

I dug in my bag for a tissue and tried to hand it to him. He just stood there sobbing. "Vic, please. I didn't mean it. C'mon, let's just keep looking for Mara," I pleaded.

"Everything okay here?"

I jumped slightly. An older white woman was looking down at us with concern. She had on a floppy straw hat and was carrying a giant shopping bag.

"We're fine," I said defensively. "I'm just talking to my brother."

Her frown deepened and she gave me a doubtful look. Vic was still crying. The woman bent toward him and said soothingly, "Is there anything I can do to help, dear?"

"You can leave us alone," I snapped, roughly grabbing Vic's arm. "Come on, Vic. We don't have time for this."

I dragged him away from the woman. *So typical*, I thought. People only interfered when their help wasn't needed. Where was she earlier this morning, when we were facing down that giant dog? Or the other night, when Quentin was freaking out—

I drew up short, and whipped my head around, then groaned, "This *cannot* be happening!"

Vic realized it at the same time I did. "Q's gone," he said in a shuddery voice.

## QUENTIN

I want to be back on the bus. Or the train. This place is noisy and crowded so crowded with people walking and pushing me and their mouths are open wide as they talk talk talk or eat. The food smells good, but it looks messy. It is like the cantina scene in Mos Eisley on Tatooine, but the ground is concrete instead of sand, and there are people everywhere, not aliens, but it is just as scary. I realize now that maybe I would not like Mos Eisley so much, and not just because of the monsters but because it is so loud and crowded.

Quiet Girl is gone. I saw her walk away while Tall Girl looked at the map. I wish I had walked away with her because she is nice and everyone else is mean. Tall Girl is mean too—she is yelling at Vic and he is crying and at first I put my hands over my ears but it is still too loud. I have to get away from it. So I go away and now they are all gone and I am being pushed by other people. I want to sit down and close my eyes and rock, I want to hit myself, but *that's not something we do anymore, Quentin, our brains are our most valued treasures!* So I keep walking until I finally find a quiet place.

It is another tent behind the tents where people are selling things. This tent has five ponies inside a metal ring (two white ponies, two brown ponies, and one that is white with brown spots). The ponies are attached to long metal poles and they walk in a circle, nice and quiet, and there are kids riding the ponies and grown-ups pointing phones at them. Some of the kids look afraid, but others are smiling, and I see Quiet Girl. She is standing on the other side of the circle watching the ponies too.

I walk over to her and she points to the ponies and says, "*Ponis*," and I nod and say, "Ponies."

We watch the ponies and they look nice, all big brown eyes and whiskers, and they are quiet, too, not loud like the dog. Quiet Girl is saying something, but I do not understand her. I decide that we can stay here until all the people go home and then we will go find Mommy when it is nice and quiet again.

But then Tall Girl appears with Loud Boy. She still looks angry. "What are you doing here?"

Quiet Girl points again and says, "*Ponis*."

"She said 'ponies,'" Loud Boy says. He looks sad, his face is wet. Tall Girl should not yell at him; it is probably not his fault that he is loud, and besides, he does helpful things like taking us to Torrance.

"Yeah, I got that. It's the same word in English," Tall Girl says. "We don't have money for a pony ride, Mara."

I look at the sign, which reads, *Pony Rides $5*.

I have five dollars. Mommy put it in a special pocket in my backpack and made me promise to keep it for *emergency purposes only*—it is not to be spent on anything else. Is this an emergency purpose? I think it might be, because when Tall Girl grabs Quiet Girl's hand, she starts to cry too. And now Loud Boy is crying and Quiet Girl is crying and people are looking at us.

I find the five dollars in my backpack and hand it to the man who is leading the ponies around. He looks at me and says, "I'm afraid you're a little too big, son."

I point to Quiet Girl and say, "Emergency."

The man's eyes crinkle at the corners as he smiles. He takes the money and says, "Well, seeing as it's an emergency, I can squeeze your friend in on the next round."

Tall Girl says, "No thanks, we've got to get going."

The man says, "Well, it only takes a few minutes. Looks like she's got her mind set on it, huh, little girl?"

Quiet Girl sniffles. She is still crying, but not as badly.

Tall Girl says, "Mara, we don't have time for this."

Then Loud Boy says, "Why can't you just let her have a pony ride? I mean, when is she ever going to get to do that again?"

Tall Girl looks at Quiet Girl, then at the ponies, then back at Quiet Girl. Finally, she makes a loud noise and says, "Fine. Then we get out of here, okay?"

The man offers his hand, and Quiet Girl takes it. He leads her to the brown pony with the white spots, which I think might be the best pony because it has the most whiskers. He lifts Quiet Girl up and when the pony starts moving she smiles bigger than I have ever seen anyone smile. She leans forward and kisses the pony on its mane and I look at Loud Boy and Tall Girl and they are smiling, too, though not as big as Quiet Girl. And I feel like maybe the emergency is over now, and we can go see Mommy as soon as the pony ride is done.

# ELEVEN

## VIC

I was kind of shocked that Nevaeh said it was okay for Mara to have that pony ride. I mean, it was almost as shocking as Q pulling a five-dollar bill out of nowhere. Had that dude been holding out on me or what? And then he just handed it to the ticket guy and said, "Emergency." Up until now he'd barely said anything to us, and suddenly he's chatting with strangers?

We watched as Mara went round and round. The pony's head bobbed as it walked, and Mara kicked its sides lightly with her heels. I swear, I'd never seen the kid so happy; her face was practically split in two, she was grinning so hard. Obviously, it was nothing like the rush that I got from riding my sweet Ducati motorcycle, but I had to admit, it looked pretty fun. I was wondering if maybe Q had more money in that magic backpack, and if he did maybe I could get a ride, too, even though almost all the other kids in line were a lot younger. But as soon as Mara climbed off and came back over to us, Nevaeh said, "Enough of this nonsense. Let's get out of here."

And that's when I saw the strand of ride tickets on the ground, like a gift from God. I scooped them up and showed Nevaeh. "Hey, check it out."

Without meeting my eyes, she asked, "What are those?"

I could tell she felt guilty for making up all those lies about my dad. And they *were* lies, just so you know. For a minute there, I thought she might be telling the truth, but then I realized it didn't make any sense. If my dad had been deported, *nothing* would've kept him from coming back for me. No, he was only still in El Salvador because he'd been captured during his mission.

Nevaeh was just angry that we'd snuck out of the house, so she kept saying mean things to get back at me. But maybe I could use that guilt. . . .

"Tickets," I said, waving to the sign nearby. "It says we can use them for rides."

Nevaeh rolled her eyes. "We're not going on any rides, Vic."

"Why not?"

"Because we can't waste the whole day here."

"Why not?"

"I have homework."

"It's Saturday."

"I have to finish my science fair project," she said, crossing her arms over her chest. "I *should* already be working on it, but instead I'm here."

"Exactly," I said. "You're here. And you'll probably never be here again, right? I mean, when do we get to go to a place like this? I'll tell you when—never."

I could see her wavering. Her eyes drifted toward the Ferris wheel, and she bit her lower lip.

"Have you ever been on a Ferris wheel before?" I asked. "Because I haven't. It can't take more than ten minutes, right? And what's ten minutes in the grand scheme of things? Especially since we never get to do anything fun."

"Fun," Q parroted.

I turned to her triumphantly. "See? Even Q wants to go."

"How many tickets do we need?" she asked doubtfully.

I counted them out and checked the sign. "We've got twenty, and it's five each for the Ferris wheel. So this is totally, like, destiny!"

"It's not destiny, Vic, just a coincidence," Nevaeh sighed. But she was wrong. When something fell in your lap like this, it obviously meant something.

Mara tugged at her hand. She was still smiling, her

eyes were all shiny as she said, "*Por favor*, Nevaeh."

Nevaeh looked at each of us, then threw up her free hand. "Okay, fine! If we ride the Ferris wheel, will you all *promise* to stick together after that?"

"Oh yeah," I said, nodding my head hard.

Q and Mara didn't say anything, but then, they pretty much never did. Nevaeh heaved another dramatic sigh and we pushed back into the crowd.

There was a line for the Ferris wheel. I could tell Nevaeh was getting antsy, so I decided to distract her; it would be a serious drag if she made us leave because it was taking too long. "So there's this guy who works in a gas station, right?"

"What guy?" Nevaeh asked, craning her head to see how many people were in front of us.

"It doesn't matter; it's a joke." Man, Nevaeh could be so thick sometimes. "Anyway, one day he's pumping gas, and another guy drives into the gas station with a car full of penguins." Mara looked confused, so I explained, "*Pingüinos*."

She nodded and smiled. I kept going. "So the gas station guy says to the driver, 'Hey, man, you should take those penguins to the zoo!' And the driver says, 'That's a great idea, thanks!' and he drives off."

"How long is this joke, exactly?" Nevaeh asked.

"Sheesh, relax. Not too long, and it's worth it, promise." We arrived at the front of the line. I handed the tickets over and the four of us climbed into the empty swing. It was a tight squeeze, but luckily we were all skinny. "Okay, so a few weeks go by. And then—"

The Ferris wheel suddenly groaned, and we swung back so fast my stomach jumped. I swallowed hard; maybe this wasn't such a great idea, considering I already felt a little sick. We stopped ten feet off the ground; our carriage swung back and forth as they let people onto the swing below us.

"Then what?" Nevaeh sounded a little nervous too, which made me feel better.

"Oh, so you want to know the end now?" It was a little hard to talk; I had a weird lump in my throat.

"Oh, I'm totally fine not knowing the end," Nevaeh said.

But Mara piped up, "*Los pingüinos!*" and even Q seemed to be paying attention for a change.

So I said, "Okay, okay. A few weeks later the gas station guy is working, and the same driver shows back up. He's still got the penguins in the back of his car, but this time, they're all wearing sunglasses. *Gafas de sol*," I explained to Mara. "And the gas station guy says, 'Hey, I thought I told you to take those penguins to the zoo!'"

The Ferris wheel lurched again, swinging us up another level. But this time, it didn't stop. We were suddenly soaring up toward the sky, higher and higher, the ground dropping away beneath us. It felt scary and awesome at the same time, and we were all gripping the bar, knuckles white.

Mara let out a little yelp as we reached the very top. We seemed to hover there for a second, weightless, then gravity tipped us forward. I raised my hands in the air and whooped as we plummeted back toward the earth. . . . It was the best rush ever, I'll admit it. Even sweeter than riding my Ducati. It felt like we were on some giant animal that was carrying us all together, and something about that gave me an even bigger lump in my throat.

Mara was laughing, and Nevaeh whooped too, so loud I could hardly believe it. Only Q didn't look happy, he was gripping the bar and his eyes were squeezed shut and I really hoped he didn't puke, because that would suck for all of us.

We went around one, two, three more times, then stopped suddenly near the top of the Ferris wheel. As the carriage rocked slightly, we all caught our breath. The people on the ground below looked tiny. It was quiet up here, and a nice cool breeze wicked the sweat off my arms and tousled my hair. I could see a police officer directing traffic away from the blocked-off streets, and then past that, another block farther. . . . I caught my breath.

White sand, then blue stretching out to the horizon.

"*La playa*," Mara said, like she was in a church. We all stared at it for a minute, then Nevaeh cleared her throat and said, "That's it?"

"What do you mean?" I asked, startled, because how could she not be impressed? I mean, I'd lived in Los Angeles my entire life, but I'd never seen the ocean before. And that view, from up high, was possibly the coolest thing ever.

"The joke."

"Oh," I said. "Right. Well, the guy says, 'I thought I told you to take those penguins to the zoo!' And the driver says, 'Oh, I did. And they *loved* it! So now I'm taking them to the beach!'"

There was a long beat, and then Nevaeh started laughing. Mara was giggling too, so maybe she'd understood the whole joke; just in case, I'd retell it to her in Spanish later.

But the most surprising thing was Q. He was shaking hard; for a second I thought he was having another attack. But then he opened his mouth and made this strange, barking noise, and I realized he was laughing. And suddenly, he did something even crazier: he yelled out, "Shred fat sue fast!" at the top of his lungs.

It sounded so weird and funny that it made the rest of us laugh harder, so hard that the carriage pitched crazily, canting almost all the way forward, then back so that we were looking at the ground, then up toward the sky. Like that moment on a swing when you're going so high, it seems like you might just loop all the way around. This was like that, but so much better.

With no warning, the Ferris wheel started moving again. It looped around three more times, until we reached the bottom. The guy running the ride lifted the safety bar and we all staggered off, barely able to stand upright. I was still laughing so hard my stomach hurt and my cheeks were sore. Q had stopped making the barking noise but he was actually smiling, and Mara was making her clown doll dance.

I turned to Nevaeh and said, "See? Fun!"

## NEVAEH

At first, I wasn't going to let Mara ride the pony. We'd wasted enough time already, and who knew how much longer it would take to get to the hospital in Torrance? Never mind the trip back home. If we were lucky, we'd make it back by dinnertime.

But then Vic said, "Why can't you just let her have a pony ride?" And both he and the pony guy were looking at me like I was some sort of terrible person. I swear even Quentin was giving me attitude. I wanted to explain that we weren't even supposed to be here, that they'd ruined *my* day . . . but then I saw Mara. She had a resigned look, like she was expecting to be disappointed. It reminded me of when my puppy was taken away. That's what our lives were, I realized: seeing the good stuff, but almost never getting to have it.

*Not this time*, I thought. I was sick of being the bad guy who always had to say no. Mara wanted a pony ride? Fine. She'd get one.

But it turned out that once you said yes to something, it became a lot easier to say it again. Which was how I suddenly found myself on a Ferris wheel for the first time in my life. I'd never really understood the point of carnival rides: Why spend the little money I had on something that would make me nauseous or scared?

And as soon as we swung off the ground, I was regretting it. We weren't at Disneyland, where the rides were probably inspected all the time; seeing the moving parts up close, I could tell that this Ferris wheel was seriously old. What if our swing just fell off, or got stuck? Quentin had his eyes squeezed shut; what if he started freaking out again? And the bar across our waists didn't seem strong enough to hold us. . . .

But then we reached the top. It was so quiet and still; the swing creaked slightly as it gently rocked back and forth. Staring straight out to the west, it took a second for me to understand what I was seeing.

The whole ocean stretched before us. The beach was like a long white ribbon, dotted with bright specks that I realized must be people. The water was a giant sprawl of shifting blue and green and gray. From this high up, it looked like you could step off the beach and just walk toward the horizon on a multicolored carpet.

It was the prettiest thing I'd ever seen. Gazing at it, I felt something swell in my stomach, a sense that maybe the world wasn't such a terrible place after all. I blinked back a few tears.

The others were all staring out, too; Vic had actually fallen silent for once. Their faces reflected the same awe and wonder I was feeling.

"*La playa*," Mara whispered.

In a voice so low it was barely a whisper, Vic murmured, "Dad would love this."

He didn't even seem to realize that he'd said it, which made me feel even worse. I bit my lip; Vic had just given me one of the best experiences of my life, despite the fact that I'd fought him every step of the way. He was the reason we were all here, instead of just getting through another tedious day in Echo Park. He was a good kid. I should try to appreciate him more.

I wanted to say all that to him, but didn't know where to start. So instead, I said, "That's it?" When he threw me a wounded look, I hurried to explain. "The joke."

"Oh." His face lit up again. To be honest, I'd probably

heard that joke a dozen times at the Welcome Center. Still, when he rattled off the punchline, I genuinely cracked up. Vic looked happy that I was laughing, which made me feel a little less guilty. Then out of nowhere Quentin made a joke too—at least, I think it was meant to be a joke. And he laughed along with us, which had to be some sort of major breakthrough or something.

When we got off the Ferris wheel, we were all still laughing, and Vic said, "See? Fun!" and I had to admit, he was right. I'd probably never had that much fun before in my entire life, which was pretty pathetic. It made me wish we could stay longer. Maybe go on more rides, or eat some food, or wander through the booths. We could spend just one day pretending to be regular kids.

But I only had a few dollars left, and we were out of tickets, and when I checked my watch it was nearly ten o'clock. Just like that, the spell was broken.

Vic met my eyes and nodded, as if silently acknowledging something. Then he clapped his hands together and said, "Okay, guys. Back to the quest!"

I was really grateful that for once, he hadn't made me be the bad guy. I went to take Mara's hand, but she surprised me (and him too, probably) by reaching for Quentin instead. He stared at their clasped hands as if they were a mystery he couldn't fathom, but he didn't let go.

The Ferris wheel was at the far end of the street

fair. We passed a couple of Porta-Potties and humming generators, stepping carefully to avoid food wrappers and other trash that people had discarded as they were leaving.

When we reached the sawhorses that marked the end of the fair, we stopped. A police car tore past, sirens blazing. A plane swooped low overhead, and a couple of pigeons fought over a hot dog bun in the gutter. I pulled out Vic's crumpled map and squinted at it, trying to pinpoint Redondo Beach (*la playa*, I thought silently). Standing here, you'd never guess that it was just a few blocks away.

The breeze we'd enjoyed at the top of the Ferris wheel was gone. The heat made my shirt stick to my back. Vic pulled a water bottle out of his pack and started to chug it. When I held out my hand, he hesitated, then handed it over. He was sweating even worse than I was: his hair was slick with it, and he was panting slightly.

"You okay?" I asked. He really did look sick. *Hopefully it's nothing contagious*, I thought as I handed the water bottle back.

"Yeah," he said, but it came out breathy, like he'd been running.

I eyed him. "You sure?"

"Just tired." He wiped the back of his hand across his forehead. "No worries, Moneypenny."

I glared at him. "I told you—"

"I know, I know. Just kidding." He handed the bottle to Mara and Quentin and said, "This is the last of it unless we find a water fountain, so make sure to share it."

"I could go back and get more," I said, waving toward the fair. I had a couple of dollars of grocery money left, and an emergency twenty that I kept a closely guarded secret. *Twenty dollars would buy more rides*, I thought wistfully.

But Vic shook his head hard. "Nope, a deal's a deal. Onward!"

"All right," I sighed. Trying to sound cheerful, like this was going to be a great adventure, I said, "Who's up for a three-mile walk?"

"I am!" Vic said, a little hoarsely. Mara and Quentin didn't say anything, but their faces fell.

I wasn't exactly looking forward to it, either, but we'd come this far. And, unexpectedly, now I kind of wanted to keep going. What if we *did* find Quentin's mother? I pictured a taller, thinner version of him, with the same fine blond hair and milky blue eyes. She'd be lying in a hospital bed wearing a long white nightgown, and when we came in she'd say, *Why, Quentin, I've been waiting for you!*

And when we explained how we'd helped him find her, she'd be so thrilled she'd offer us each a hug. Then she'd kiss my cheek and say, "Thank you, Nevaeh, for bringing my boy back to me."

I knew that was as unlikely as one of Vic's fantasies; for all we knew, she might not even be at the hospital. Quentin wasn't exactly the most reliable source of information. But if there was even a chance, well . . . maybe this was a righteous quest after all, just like Vic kept saying.

We started walking. Vic fell in step beside me, and Quentin and Mara trailed close behind. I kept checking back to make sure they didn't wander off again.

Vic mumbled something.

"What?" I asked, checking the map again to make sure we were headed the right way.

Louder, he said, "You called me your brother. When you were talking to that lady."

"Oh yeah," I said. "So?"

"So . . . it was kind of nice." Vic stared at his feet, scuffing them along the sidewalk. "Hey, we're still only a couple of blocks from the beach. Maybe there's even a boardwalk or something like that. Might be a nicer place to walk, if it's going in the same direction."

"Don't press your luck, Vic," I muttered, cuffing him lightly on the shoulder. He grinned, still not meeting my eyes. I briefly toyed with the idea of taking a detour by the beach. It wouldn't be that far out of our way. But they'd probably get covered in sand, and how would I explain that to Mrs. K when we got back? No, the view from the Ferris wheel would have to be enough.

As we walked, the blocks of stores gradually gave way to houses tucked behind hedges. They weren't big and fancy, but still looked nicer than the ones in our neighborhood. They were mostly stucco painted in shades of beige, with perfectly trimmed lawns sloping down toward the sidewalk. I wondered if Quentin had lived in a house like that with his mom.

The walk actually wasn't so bad; something about being in a different place let my thoughts wander. I felt calm and relaxed; I realized that usually, I was only thinking of the next thing I had to do, the next place I had to be. I constantly had a tight little ball in the pit of my stomach, put there by the endless list of chores droning on in my head: laundry, dishes, homework, lunches, vacuuming . . . but maybe because I couldn't do any of those things right now, even if I wanted to, that voice had fallen silent.

I glanced back: Quentin and Mara were shuffling along a couple yards behind us. The cuffs of Mara's pajama bottoms were black, and there were chocolate stains on her top; I'd have to sneak in a load of laundry before bedtime and hope they washed out.

I sighed. Maybe there was no getting away from the list after all.

Vic was dragging too. I slowed to let him catch up, then asked, "How do you know his mom's at this hospital, anyway?"

He was huffing slightly, and pouring sweat. For someone who always bragged about being in "peak physical condition," he seemed to be having an awfully hard time today.

"There's only one hospital in Torrance," Vic panted. "I checked."

"Really?"

"Yeah," he said, sounding affronted. "Why? You don't believe me?"

"I'm just surprised, is all." Off his look, I added, "Let's face it, you're not exactly known for your planning skills."

Vic bridled. "Are you kidding? Before I go on a mission, I spend *weeks* researching it."

"Sure you do, Vic." I sighed. Just when he was starting to seem somewhat normal, he came out with a ridiculous statement like that.

There was a long pause, then he said, "I know you don't like me very much."

"What? That's ridiculous. Of course I like you."

"No, you don't. But it's cool," he said. "I get it."

The matter-of-fact way he said it made it even worse. Especially because he was right. Up until today, I'd only thought of him as an annoyance, someone who added more work to my to-do list. Which was pretty awful, now that I thought about it. No wonder he lived in a fantasy world: we'd never given him a reason to join us in the real one. At least, I hadn't.

"I wouldn't do it, you know," he said out of nowhere.

"Do what?" I asked, checking on Quentin and Mara again. They plodded along with their gazes on the sidewalk like a pair of dogs. They didn't look unhappy, though. And they were still holding hands.

"Spy on you for Mrs. K."

"I know you wouldn't." We reached an intersection, and I double-checked the map. "We have to take a left onto Calle Mayor," I said. "Stay close while we're crossing."

The light turned, and I led them across the street. Calle Mayor was a lot like the street we'd just come from: beige houses with hedges that separated them from the sidewalk. *People must get lost a lot around here*, I thought.

Vic kicked at a pebble on the sidewalk and sent it skittering into the street. "And I didn't mean to tell on Mario. It was an accident, sort of."

Vic launched into a long explanation of what had happened with Mario. It involved candy and dentists and Ms. Judy from DCFS. I only half listened, because I was still distracted by what he'd said about me not liking him. I wondered if Mara felt the same way. I did things for them, but only because I had to. And never anything fun, because that wasn't on the list.

I decided that when we got home, I wouldn't work on my science fair project after all. I'd use my emergency money to take them out for ice cream. There was a place a few blocks from our house, where we could sit on a bench outside and eat our cones. The ice cream would run all over Mara's hand, so I'd have to make sure to get extra napkins, and . . . something Vic said suddenly penetrated, and I frowned. "Wait, what?"

"I said, Mario would've had to leave soon anyway."

"Why?" I asked, doing another quick check on Mara and Quentin. Mara was carrying on a long, one-sided conversation in Spanish. Quentin looked like he was listening, even though he couldn't possibly understand what she was saying. Or could he? Who knew, maybe he spoke Spanish too. *He's full of surprises*, I thought with what I realized, surprisingly, was affection.

"Mario was going into high school soon," Vic said, as if that explained it.

"So?" I asked. I'd be starting ninth grade in the fall. I'd already mapped out how long it would take to get from Belmont High to Logan for afternoon pickup.

Vic wore an oddly unreadable expression. "Well, once you start high school, Mrs. K kicks you out."

It took a minute for the words to register. "No, she doesn't."

"Yeah, she does," Vic said matter-of-factly. "Once you hit high school, she sends you away. That's what happened to Silvia, and Anya . . ."

And just like that, the bottom dropped out of my world. I stopped dead and said, "What?"

Vic got this look on his face, like he suddenly realized he'd said something wrong. "Didn't you know? I thought—"

"You're lying."

"No, I'm not," he said defensively. "I think that's why Mario took stuff: 'cause he knew it didn't really matter anyway."

I stared at Vic. He looked worried, and he was sweating even harder. Maybe he was just trying to get back at me for what I'd said about his dad. "Ms. Judy wouldn't allow that," I insisted.

Vic shrugged. "She's always complaining about how hard it is to find good foster parents. So maybe she doesn't have a choice."

I didn't want to believe it, but it all made a horrible kind of sense. And it explained why there were no hand-me-downs in my size, even though there were boxes for Mara and Vic.

Everything I'd done, all the cleaning and cooking and lunches and baths: none of it mattered. And the things I'd missed out on—hanging out at Aliyah's house, or window-shopping with Jada, or just . . . anything. The things the other kids in my class got to experience, but not me. I'd missed it all. And for what? If I'd known the truth, I wouldn't have tried so hard.

As if from a great distance, I heard Mara ask, "*¿Qué pasa?*" They were all staring at me. Waiting for me to take care of them, the way I always did.

A wave of anger and frustration and panic rose inside me, blurring my vision. I had to get away. From Vic and Quentin and Mara, from Mrs. K, from everyone who wanted something from me or asked too much or just hadn't cared.

So I turned and ran as fast and hard as I could.

Vic called after me, but I wasn't about to stop, not for him or anyone else. I vaulted off the sidewalk and into the street, determined to escape. I would keep running forever, because if I went far enough and fast enough, maybe I'd finally find a place to belong. I pictured my fantasy apartment, the sleek walls and floors, the silence, and thought, *Yes, that's where I'll go.* Which was ridiculous, but it was like I'd stepped into a dream, and anything was possible as long as I kept moving forward. *Six weeks to the end of school*, I thought. *Four years to college. Three years to medical school . . .*

The sound of blaring horns abruptly penetrated my fog. I skidded to a stop, which was a mistake because as soon as I did, the real world came rushing back in.

## QUENTIN

Tall Girl and Loud Boy have stopped walking. They are talking, and Tall Girl looks unhappy and Loud Boy is sweaty and my feet are tired and it is taking a long time to get to the hospital. I hope we are not lost again.

Quiet Girl is not so quiet after all, now she does not stop talking, but in Spanish (like Dora!), so I do not mind it so much. She has a soft voice and it sounds a little like a bird singing, so I listen and sometimes I nod and Quiet Girl (Talking Girl?) seems happy. Her hand is smaller than mine. I do not like to hold hands, but she is very small and maybe if I let go there will be another emergency, and I have no more money to fix it, so I do not let go.

I can tell that we are close to home. This street looks like our street, even though it is not our street (619 Maple Avenue, like the tree). We are not going to the house, though, we are going to the hospital, and I hate the hospital. It is loud in a bad way (machines that beep, phones that ring, people crying. And a bad smell, different from Pink Lips Lady's car but still *could use a spritz of lavender!*).

But Mommy is there and maybe now she is okay and she can take me back to the house and everything will be waiting: my R2-D2 alarm clock and the computer and the little bottles lined up on the kitchen table in a neat row, filled with different pills all shapes and sizes (*I don't want to talk about those, Quentin; they're Mommy's business*).

I do not know why Tall Girl is upset again. She was happy on the Ferris wheel (the Ferris wheel! Up and up, so high, much higher than our house, and from there you could see the ocean! I was afraid at first, but then the rocking was nice—it was like we were all rocking together, and then Vic told a confusing story about penguins and laughed and I understood that it was a joke, so I told my joke and they laughed even harder! I wish Mommy had been there to laugh, too). But now Tall Girl looks angry and sad at the same time, and then she turns and suddenly she is running, running away from us, and I am confused because are we all supposed to run, will we run all the way to the hospital? But no, she is running into the street, and that is *not safe; one must look both ways, and even then, make sure to cross with the light, not against it!*

There are cars coming very fast, a lot of them like they are in a race, and in the middle of the road Tall

Girl stops moving. Tall Girl stands there like she is a rock and they are a river and they will have to go around her, but they do not—instead, there are loud squeaks and squeals and horns—it is suddenly so loud, much too loud. I do not like it at all.

Even Quiet Girl yells, "Nevaeh!" and that startles me, so I let go of her hand. Loud Boy is not yelling, he is not talking at all. He falls down and he is on the ground, lying on the sidewalk as if he has decided to go to sleep even though it is not nighttime and I do not understand because he has not been hit by a car, not like Tall Girl, and people are still yelling and it is too much, all too much, and I cannot help it, I start to *hit hit hit* to make it all go away.

# TWELVE

## VIC

I could tell right away that I'd said the wrong thing. I'd just kind of figured that Nevaeh already knew she'd have to leave this summer. I mean, she's so smart, and she always acts like she knows everything.

But she hadn't known. I was kind of surprised she got so upset about it, though; I mean, it's not like she ever seemed happy to be at Mrs. K's. Maybe somewhere else, she wouldn't have to do so much cooking and cleaning. Maybe they'd find her a place with older kids that she liked better than us.

But she got this look that scared me. I'd seen Nevaeh look angry, irritated, annoyed, impatient . . . basically, all different variations on mad. But this was different. Her whole face kind of froze, like she couldn't even process what I was saying. Then it went slack, her eyes got blank, and her mouth opened slightly. Like she was turning into a zombie or something. It was so weird that I stepped back, a tiny voice in my head warning that she might bite or hit or kick me.

Instead, she stared at me, then looked at Q and Mara. Then she turned and started running.

I yelled for her to stop, but she acted like she didn't hear me, and she ran straight out into the street! It was like one of those nightmares where something really horrible was happening, but you couldn't do anything to stop it, so instead you just watched while everything fell apart. Like with the dog, but so much worse.

The street had been empty, but a light must've changed down the road, because out of nowhere there were suddenly tons of cars, and they all looked huge as they headed straight for Nevaeh. She'd frozen right in the middle of the street, as if she'd hit an invisible wall or something. She was crying, but silently. I was thinking it was strange that I'd never seen her cry before, when what I should've been thinking, should've been *doing*, was using my mad skills to dash into traffic and yank her to safety. And then I'd be a hero, and my picture would be in the paper above the headline "Local Boy Saves His Sister!" and then everyone would know that I was a really cool, special kid who no one should ever leave behind.

Car brakes were squealing, like the drivers had finally realized that the girl wasn't going to get out of the way, that she was just going to stand there until they hit her. It was too late, though, they were too close, and finally my legs started working again and I ran toward her. I pictured myself leaping high into the air and landing on the hood of the closest car, then leaping onto another hood until I reached her, pushing her out of the way just in time. I'd do a double somersault and land on my feet and everyone would applaud wildly.

The problem was that before I even reached the street, everything suddenly went sideways on me. It felt like a thousand hands pushing at the same time, throwing me to the ground.

I lay there and all I could see were tires and all I could hear were grown-ups screaming and Mara screaming and Q making some sort of awful howling sound, and I wanted to tell them all to shut up and go help Nevaeh. But my mouth wasn't working properly; it would only open and close like I'd turned into a fish or something. And I was so tired. I mean, I'd been feeling pretty tired all day, but this was something else, like I didn't even have enough energy left to move a finger. I really wanted to save Nevaeh, but suddenly I realized that in spite of all my training, I wasn't even going to be able to save myself.

●●●

# NEVAEH

When my mind snapped back into place, I was standing in the middle of the street. It was bizarre. One second I was beside Vic on the sidewalk, the next I was staring at cars barreling toward me. People were shouting at me; Mara's tiny voice rose above the others, and it had a panicked note that I'd never heard before. Quentin was howling and hitting himself, the same way he had that first night. And Vic . . .

Vic was lying on the ground. He looked dead.

A horn blared. I spun around and saw a line of cars bearing down on me, fast. They were braking, but I could tell it was too late. That shook me out of my stupor. I ran away from the cars, angling toward the sidewalk. . . .

My lungs burned and my feet hurt from slapping hard against the pavement, but I was making it, I was almost clear . . .

. . . and then a hard shove from behind sent me flying forward.

I landed hard, the wind forced out of my body. I felt sharp stabs of pain everywhere, like I was being pierced by a thousand knives at the same time.

Abruptly, there was silence. I was lying flat on my stomach, and everything hurt.

A woman's face swam into view: she was older, white, and for a confusing moment I thought it might be the same lady from the street fair. But no, she wasn't wearing a hat, and she was heavier and had on a lot of makeup.

"Honey, you okay?" she asked loudly.

I groaned and tried to get up. She waved her arms frantically at me. "Hold on there, hold on now, don't move. . . ."

"The kids," I muttered. "Gotta check on them."

I pushed off the ground and slowly got to my hands and knees.

"I really think you should stay still," the woman barked at me. "I called nine-one-one, and there's an ambulance coming. . . ."

"I'm fine, I think," I said.

"Is she okay? Why was she in the middle of the road?" A small crowd was gathering, talking at me or to each other; I wished they'd all just shut up. I cautiously got to my feet, which provoked another flurry of gasps and protests. My jeans were torn, my knees bloody beneath them. My elbows were ripped up pretty badly, too. But nothing seemed broken, and my head felt fine, which had to be some sort of miracle.

"Excuse me," I said to the tight knot of people clustered around me. "My brother," I tried to explain as I lurched toward the sidewalk. My legs were still wobbly, as if someone had spun me around in the air instead of hurling me through it. I flashed back on the Ferris wheel and swallowed hard. "I need to go, please. . . ."

The crowd parted reluctantly, letting me stagger forward. Every step announced a new pain: my right knee was swelling up, and my left ankle felt sprained. I gritted my teeth and hobbled away while they all watched. No one seemed to have connected me to the three children on the sidewalk, but now that I was headed for them, a murmur built up around me. Someone said, "What's wrong with him?" And someone else said, "Which one?" because Quentin was still beating himself on the head and Vic was lying on the ground twitching. Mara swayed between them, shoulders shaking with sobs as she hiccuped my name over and over again: "Ne-vay-ya, Ne-vay-ya."

There was the high, shrill shriek of sirens approaching. My thoughts were all scrambled up inside my brain, like it was one of the clunky, old computers at school that crashed all the time and took forever to reboot. *Mara is upset, but not hurt*, I thought, struggling to take inventory. Quentin . . . well, there wasn't much I could do for Quentin at the moment. Vic was obviously in the worst shape.

When I reached him, I made the mistake of dropping to my knees and instantly gasped with pain. I awkwardly adjusted until I was sitting on my right hip, which was a little better.

Vic's eyes were closed, and his chest was rising and

falling much too quickly. I wasn't sure what to do. Should I shake him? Or just leave him alone?

I rubbed his arm and said, "Vic? Can you hear me?"

Mara put a small hand on my shoulder and said, "What eez wrong with Vic?"

It took a second to realize that I'd actually understood her for a change because she'd asked in English. I said, "I don't know. Can you try to help Quentin?"

Mara nodded solemnly and went over to where Quentin was rocking and hitting himself. She very slowly and carefully reached out and touched his head. I winced, expecting him to lash out at her, but instead his rocking slowed. She touched him again, gently, the way you would a nervous cat, and he fell still. She kept talking to him in a low voice until he finally stopped moaning.

I turned my attention back to Vic. He was pale, and his eyes were still shut. I carefully drew his head onto my lap and stroked his hair; it was damp with sweat, like he'd been running a race. He was breathing hard, like he was battling something the rest of us couldn't see.

A screech of tires as an ambulance pulled up to the curb. As the paramedics forced their way through the crowd, I said, "It's all going to be okay, Vic. I promise."

• • •

# QUENTIN

At first I do not want to get in the ambulance, but there are many people on the street who look angry and the ambulance is clean. They put Loud Boy on the special bed that fits inside. Tall Girl and Quiet Girl get into the ambulance and so does a man in a blue uniform. It is crowded but not as crowded as outside.

I do not like ambulances. Mommy and me rode in an ambulance once, and it was no fun at all, not even when they put on the sirens and we raced around all the other cars as fast as we could go.

Loud Boy looks like he is asleep, but I know he is not, because even when he sleeps he talks. He moves around a lot in his sleep, too, but now he does not move at all.

The ambulance man is attaching wires to Loud Boy, until he looks like C-3PO after he was blasted to pieces in *Stars Wars: Episode V—The Empire Strikes Back*. In Cloud City, Chewbacca tried to put C-3PO back together, but he did not do a good job. I hope Ambulance Man will do a better job with Loud Boy.

"What's wrong with him?" Tall Girl asks.

"Not sure," Ambulance Man says. "Looks like he fainted. Is he on any medication?"

"Yeah, for ADHD," Tall Girl says.

"That might explain it, then," Ambulance Man says. "Especially in this heat. His pulse is good. Not much else I can do right now, but the fluids should help. And we'll get him checked out." Tall Girl seems happy when he says that, and I feel better, too. Even though the boy is loud, he is also brave and funny and I want him to wake up and be okay.

We all watch Loud Boy. Quiet Girl is next to me; she sucks on her thumb. Tall Girl's hands are shaking and her pants are torn and she has blood on her knees and elbows. Ambulance Man asks, "What happened to you?"

Tall Girl says, "One of the cars hit me, but I don't think it's too bad."

The man frowns at this and makes her sit on the edge of the bed, which is okay because Loud Boy has left lots of room at the bottom. Ambulance Man checks her knees and elbows and asks a lot of questions and says, "You were lucky; it could've been a lot worse." Then he cleans off the blood and puts on some ointment and Band-Aids and I remember Mommy did that when I fell in the parking lot in front of the grocery store (*Goodness, Quentin, you need to watch where you're going! Haste makes waste!*) and I feel like crying again.

"Where are we going?" Tall Girl asks.

"Torrance Memorial. Not far now," Ambulance Man says.

*Torrance Memorial!* I say, "Mommy!" out loud and Ambulance Man looks at me strangely, but Tall Girl smiles at me and says, "Looks like we made it after all."

# THIRTEEN

## VIC

When I was six years old, we lived in Tía Maria's garage because there wasn't room in the house. My aunt was pregnant with her fourth kid, and the oldest was almost exactly my age. I got along great with all my cousins, especially Alberto. We'd play manhunt and spy, and I didn't really mind sleeping in the garage. I mean, it smelled like gas, but Dad and me were on army cots next to each other, and he said it would toughen me up and put hair on my chest.

At first, it was great. My dad went out every morning to look for work, but if he couldn't find any (and he usually couldn't), he'd come home and spend the day with me instead, which was awesome. There was this park by the house where we'd play soccer with a bunch of other dads and their kids. My dad was so good, everyone wanted him on their team; he joked that he could've gone pro if he'd stayed in El Salvador. When I asked why he'd left, though, he'd say he didn't like to talk about it. He said it was better in California, and I was lucky I was born here because it meant I'd never have to leave. I thought El Salvador sounded pretty great, though, and maybe if we lived there we would've had a house all to ourselves.

Sometimes I couldn't sleep because it got cold in the garage and there were strange noises outside, animals rooting through the garbage cans and once a terrifying yapping noise that Tío Carlos said was coyotes. I asked if they ate kids and he said, "Only bad ones," and the way he was looking at me made it pretty obvious who he meant, although I never did anything bad on purpose. Things just seemed to break around me; I'd be holding something, and then it would be in pieces in my hand. I was always sorry, but no one ever believed it was an accident. Tía Maria would say, "What's the matter with you, Victorio?" and, "Ay, you're like Cipitío," who my dad said was an imaginary troublemaker with backward feet (I thought that actually sounded pretty cool, and Dad said in El Salvador he was kind of a hero for kids, anyway).

My dad also said that Tía Maria had always been a pain, even when my mother was alive, but we had to be extra nice because if she kicked us out, we'd have nowhere to go. I promised to do my best, but she only seemed to notice my mistakes, never the good stuff. Dad said that was probably because I looked so much like my mom, it made Maria miss her even more. I told him that didn't make sense, and he said sometimes people couldn't help how they acted. Talking about Mom made him sad, too, so then I always changed the subject.

My mother died when I was a baby. No one ever explained how, exactly, but that also seemed to be my fault. The only picture I'd seen was of her and Tía Maria when they were both teenagers. They had their arms around each other and my mother was laughing. Tía Maria was actually thin back then, but she still wasn't as pretty as my mom. Mom had black hair and brown eyes, like mine. You could tell by her smile that she was funny and I bet everyone had liked her. If she'd lived, she definitely would've been the kind of mom who never stopped hugging and kissing you, even when it was totally embarrassing (not that I'd be embarrassed; I'd even let her hold my hand as she walked me to school).

For hours every night, I'd lie awake on my cot, listening to my dad snore. To pass the time, I'd make up stories about all the cool stuff my mom and me would've done together. Like going to Legoland, where we ate ice cream out of waffle cones and rode every ride until it was dark out. Then she bought me a hot dog for dinner and didn't mind when I got ketchup all over the car on the ride home.

Or another time, we went to the beach and rented bicycles and rode along the boardwalk until we were hot and tired. Then we played in the waves and built a sandcastle that looked real, with turrets and everything. Or another time, we went for a picnic but it started raining, and Mom just laughed (because she was never angry or upset; she always saw the best in everything) and said, "What fun! We can make mud pies!" and we did that, then threw them at each other (although I was careful not to hit her; I didn't want her to get dirty) and then we splashed in puddles and she got muddy anyway, but she didn't care because she was the best, kindest, most understanding mom ever.

I never told anyone about these stories; not my dad, not even my cousin Alberto. Partly because I didn't want them making fun of me (sometimes the kids at school teased me, saying my mom wasn't dead, she'd left because I was so ugly). But also because I realized that if I kept the stories to myself, they became more real. It was like this whole other world I could step into, one that was so much better than living in a garage with a dad who, after a while, was always too tired to talk or play soccer anymore. The stories about my mom were special; they belonged to me.

Then one day, my dad didn't come home at all. Tía

Maria and Tío Carlos had a lot of whispered conversations that stopped as soon as I came in the room. If I asked when Dad was coming home, they'd tell me to go play outside with my cousins. For weeks I slept in the garage by myself, always waiting for Dad to rush in and grab me in a big hug and tell me he was sorry. But there was nothing but the usual night noises outside.

Then Alberto and I got in a fight over something dumb when we were walking home from school one afternoon, and he started yelling that my dad got deported back to El Salvador and was never coming home. I called him a liar and pushed him, and he fell funny and broke his arm. I was really sorry, but even though I kept telling Tía Maria that, a few days later she took me aside and said that a nice lady was coming for me. She said she was sorry, too, but she couldn't handle another mouth to feed. And I didn't mind so much, because Alberto wasn't speaking to me and no one else in the house seemed to like me anymore. Plus I was taking my mother with me, in a way, and that was all that mattered.

The DCFS lady before Ms. Judy drove me to Mrs. K's house, where I had a real bed, in a real bedroom. Which was a nice change, but I missed my dad. I just kept telling myself that he'd come back for me soon.

But he didn't. I turned eight, then nine, and I never saw him or Tía Maria or Alberto or any of them again.

The garage started to feel like it had never been real.

As I got older, the stories changed. In the new ones, I rescued my mom from a burning building. I dove in to save her when she was being swept out to sea. I fought off a coyote that snuck into our picnic. Neither of us ever got hurt, of course, and afterward Mom would embrace me and say, "You are the strongest, smartest, best boy, Vic!" and she'd shower me with kisses and then we'd have chocolate cake with chocolate frosting.

I still went over those stories every once in a while, but over the years they seemed to wear as thin as my T-shirts. It got harder and harder to picture my mom. Which made me sad at first, but then other stories took over. In the new stories, I was a spy saving my dad, and that was better, right? I mean, he was still alive, so it made a lot more sense when you really thought about it. And from what he'd always said about El Salvador, it was pretty dangerous, with lots of gangs and stuff, so pretending that he'd gone back on purpose to fight them kind of made sense.

Look, I know I'm not a superspy. I know that there's no Commander Baxter or DEEC. But imagining that they're real makes me happy. Without them, I'm just a skinny kid with no friends and a family who gave him away. And who'd want to be that?

The weird thing was, when Nevaeh and me were walking together, I actually thought about telling her one of my mom stories. It seemed like she'd understand.

But then I was lying on the sidewalk, and my whole body felt like it was set in stone—I couldn't control it no matter how hard I tried. And the world kept fading in and out; I'd see bright red flowers, so close I could make out the pollen dotting the petals. A second later, the flowers were far away again, looking like they were being eaten by the vines they rested on.

Then a lady appeared.

She had straight dark hair, a little longer than mine, and sad eyes. She was wearing jeans and a pink shirt, and there was light shining all over her, so she was brighter than everything else, even the flowers. She looked really familiar.

The lady sat next to me and took my hand. And as soon as she said, "*Te quiero, mi Victorio,*" I knew that this was my real mom. Her hand was warm and soft and so light it felt like a feather. She got blurry again, but this time it was because I was crying, and she told me not to be sad. She said a bunch of other stuff about how she missed me, but she was always with me, and she was proud of me and thought I was amazing. And it was nothing like in my stories, I could tell that this was actually happening—she was really there.

Her lips brushed my forehead and she said, "*Te quiero,*" again, and I tried to tell her that I loved her, too, but she was already gone.

It was only after I woke up that I realized my dad never came.

# NEVAEH

Vic looked so small lying on the gurney. If it wasn't for the machine beeping out his pulse, I wouldn't have believed he was alive. Even though the ambulance guy said he'd be okay, I was worried; he still hadn't opened his eyes, or said anything. *This is probably the longest he's ever gone without talking*, I thought, and made a noise that was somewhere between a laugh and a cry.

I felt awful—this was all my fault. I'd told Vic over and over that remembering to take the ADHD pills was his job. His only job, really. But still—I should've reminded him. If I had, this never would've happened.

As soon as the ambulance stopped, the rear doors opened and people in scrubs pulled out the gurney and took Vic away. We were led into a waiting room that was clearly meant for sick kids and their parents; there were broken toys and torn picture books and walls painted with what looked like wilting flowers. A stern-faced nurse came over and asked a bunch of questions. I swallowed hard and gave her Mrs. K's number. *After all, what's she going to do?* I thought darkly. *Kick me out?* Apparently, I only had a couple of months left anyway. I wondered idly if she'd keep me through the summer, or kick me out the day after eighth-grade graduation.

The nurse came back with a clipboard and a bunch of forms for me to fill out. I didn't know the answer to a lot of the questions, like when Vic's birthday was. February? March, maybe? I vaguely remembered him talking about getting a cupcake at school. What did it say about me, that I'd been living with someone for almost a year and didn't know one of the most important things about him? Nothing good, I suspected.

I struggled to remember how to spell Mrs. K's full name, too: Kuznetsov. I got a sinking feeling in my stomach as I wrote it down on the forms. Soon there would be someone new in my place—someone younger, probably. And what then? Would Vic start cooking dinner and doing laundry?

It was more likely that today would be the final straw for Mrs. K, and she'd kick us all out. At least then we'd all be back in the Welcome Center together for a little while.

I handed in the forms. More people in scrubs came and went; none of them said anything to us. Mara had curled up in her chair and was fast asleep, her thumb still tucked in her mouth. I'd been trying to get her to stop sucking it for months; I'd told her it would ruin her teeth, even threatened to put nasty-tasting stuff on it (though I never had. So I wasn't that bad, right?). Now

I was half tempted to jam a thumb in my mouth too.

Quentin was sitting bolt upright, like a spaniel who'd caught a scent. It was the most alert I'd ever seen him. *Right*, I remembered. *The "quest."* I sighed and asked, "Quentin, what's your mother's name?"

He stared at me for a minute, then said, "Knox."

"Okay," I said. "And her first name?"

"Emma," he said softly.

"Great." Emma Knox sounded like a TV mom, the kind who wore aprons and baked pies from scratch and told you bedtime stories. Certainly not the sort I'd had any experience with.

I walked up to the desk where I'd dropped the forms. The nurse seemed aggravated, answering the constantly ringing phone with a sharp "Yes?" and shuffling papers as if they were misbehaving. I could empathize. "Excuse me, ma'am?"

She barked, "What?" without even glancing at me.

"I was wondering . . . I think my friend's mother is in this hospital." (I nearly said "brother," but got a flash of Vic saying that had sounded nice, which made me feel awful all over again.)

"And?" she said (more angry shuffling as she shoved Vic's forms into a folder).

"And he'd like to visit her for a minute. I can go with him; it's been a long time since he's seen her, and he really misses her."

The nurse looked up at me with a puzzled expression, as if until that moment she'd been completely unaware that there were three children sitting across from her. Her eyes softened slightly, but she said, "You can't go up there unattended."

We were basically always "unattended," I wanted to say, but instead asked, "Can you just tell us what room she's in, then? Maybe we can see her before we leave. When someone comes for us." I tried to look earnest and trustworthy, although I suspected I just looked tired.

The nurse heaved a sigh and said, "Name?"

My heart jumped. "Knox. Emma Knox."

She pounded out the name on her keyboard. Frowning at the screen, she said, "No one registered here under that name."

"Are you sure? Can you check again?" Out of the corner of my eye, I saw Quentin. He was half out of his seat with eagerness, a hopeful look on his face. Were we in the wrong hospital? Vic had said there was only one in Torrance, but maybe he'd been wrong.

"There *was* a patient under that name," the nurse said, scrolling through. Her face suddenly shuttered, and her eyes flicked back to Quentin. "Better wait for your guardian; she'll be here soon." She turned away and made a big show out of shuffling more papers.

I stood there for another minute, waiting for her to

explain, but she resolutely avoided my eyes.

I shuffled back to the seats and sat down. The expression on Quentin's face was killing me. I went to take his hand, then decided against it; Mara seemed to be the only one allowed to touch him, and she was fast asleep. "Sorry," I said. "She's not here."

His brow crinkled. "No Mommy?"

"No Mommy," I said, mentally adding, *No mommies anywhere, for any of us.* It sounded like a bad song, or a poem on a standardized test. Yesterday, I probably would've added, *Suck it up,* but instead I repeated, "Sorry."

Quentin caved into himself, crossing his arms over his chest and collapsing back against his pack.

I couldn't blame him; I felt the same way. If his mom had been here, it would've redeemed everything we'd been through today; it might've even made dealing with Mrs. K easier. Instead, our "quest" had turned out to be just another disappointment. Which shouldn't have surprised me. Getting your hopes up was always a mistake.

There was a commotion in the doorway as our case-worker, Ms. Judy, suddenly appeared. She was wearing yoga tights and a tank top, like she'd been interrupted during a workout. Strands of hair had slipped free of her sloppy bun, and she wore her usual expression of harried concern, like she was late for something. Of course, today she kind of was.

"Nevaeh! I have to say, I'm surprised," she scolded. She took us all in and her frown deepened. "God, what happened to your knees and elbows? Are you okay?"

I shrunk down in my chair, embarrassed. "I'm fine. I just fell." Would they tell her I ran into traffic? Hopefully not. I wasn't trying to kill myself, but that's probably what they'd think. They wouldn't understand that my body had just kind of taken over. The last thing I needed was to be stuck in mandatory therapy. "Where's Mrs. K?"

"She was too upset to drive. And I can't say I blame her." Ms. Judy puffed out a breath of air indignantly. Her pink lipstick was smeared as always. "Honestly, Nevaeh, Torrance? I mean . . ." She waved her arms around wildly. "Torrance?"

She said it like we'd turned up on Mars or something. I felt a little badly for Ms. Judy. It was probably her day off, and she'd been looking forward to a nice yoga class and whatever else people like her did on Saturdays—a farmers' market, maybe, or a trip to the beach. Remembering the golden strip of sand we'd seen from the top of the Ferris wheel, I felt a twinge. I should've taken them there. In the end, what difference would it have made? We were in trouble anyway.

Mara shifted in her chair and sleepily opened her eyes, stifling a yawn. The creepy clown was looking seriously worse for wear after the day's adventures.

"Vic?" Mara asked in her tiny voice.

"He'll be all right, sweetie. He just forgot to take his medicine for a few days." Ms. Judy threw me a reproving look. "Why is Mara in her pajamas?"

Defensively, I said, "She snuck out after Vic. I was trying to bring them all home." (*At least, I was at first,* I added silently.) "Anyway, I got Vic his medicine. He just forgot to take it."

"It's not your responsibility, Nevaeh. Mrs. Kuznetsov should've done a better job of monitoring that." Ms. Judy plunked down in the chair next to me, suddenly looking exhausted. "They're giving it to him now with some fluids. He should be fine soon." She shook her head. "I honestly don't know what you were thinking. I mean, *Torrance*, of all places?"

I wanted to tell her that there was a great street fair with ponies and a Ferris wheel just down the road. Instead, I said, "We were on a quest."

It sounded silly and childish. I couldn't really blame her for gaping at me. "A quest?"

"To find Quentin's mom," I said. "She's sick."

A whole flood of emotions crossed Ms. Judy's face, and suddenly I understood why Quentin's mom wasn't here anymore. I glanced at him. He was still staring at the floor, looking sad and deflated. Ms. Judy's gaze followed mine, then her lips pursed. She abruptly got to her feet and motioned for me to join her at the far end of the waiting room.

I didn't really want to, didn't want to hear it spoken out loud. But I followed her anyway.

"So?" I asked reluctantly.

"Cancer," Ms. Judy said, lowering her voice to a whisper. "She"—Ms. Judy threw a surreptitious glance at Quentin—"*succumbed* a few weeks ago."

"And no one told him?" I said, matching her voice so Quentin wouldn't hear.

"Of course he was told!" Ms. Judy said defensively. "But with his Asperger's, it wasn't clear how much he understood."

"But wasn't he at her funeral?" I asked, confused.

"The therapist thought the funeral might upset him, and since there was no other family, it wasn't even really a service, more of a . . ." Ms. Judy waved a hand, as if there were no words for it. "Apparently his mother was a bit . . . off. The neighbors said she always claimed to have come from a wealthy family, and in her will she left Quentin to her parents. But when we tracked them down, they'd never even heard of her. Turns out she grew up in the foster system herself. It's sad, really." Ms. Judy suddenly looked abashed. "I probably shouldn't have told you that."

I crossed my arms over my chest, where an ache had sprouted again. Poor Quentin. "Where's his mom buried?"

172

"She was cremated." Ms. Judy looked sad. "We weren't even sure Quentin could talk; she home-schooled him, so we didn't have any records. He's barely said a word since we collected him."

*Collected him*, like he was a thing, not a person. I looked at Quentin. Mara was talking to him again, her soft voice pattering on in Spanish, but his gaze was focused entirely on us. He obviously knew *something* was going on.

"So he wasn't there when she died?" I asked.

"No," Ms. Judy said. "He'd already been taken to the center, and we didn't realize . . . well, it's probably for the best anyway."

*Is it?* I wondered. My mom had died when I was too young to understand, but Quentin was almost eleven. That was probably it, I realized. Vic had stories; I had my future house; maybe this was Quentin's coping mechanism. Maybe he just needed to say goodbye.

"He's on a list for more therapy," Ms. Judy said defensively. "There's just a long wait. You know how these things are."

Yeah, I knew. Quentin would be lucky if they got him in before Christmas, and even then, a lot of the DCFS therapists were useless. I saw one once who spent every session telling me about her cats. All that did was make me even sadder about not having a pet of my own.

I remembered the way that Quentin had solemnly

dug into his backpack for money so that Mara could ride a pony, and his strange, barking laugh on the Ferris wheel. "No other family," Ms. Judy had said, but she was wrong. He had a new family now.

And just like that, I knew what I had to do. As if the fates agreed, Ms. Judy chose that moment to say, "I ran straight here from yoga. Can you watch them for a sec while I use the restroom?"

"Go ahead," I said blithely. "We'll be fine on our own."

## QUENTIN

I can tell that something bad has happened, because Tall Girl looks very serious. Pink Lips Lady came, and she also looks serious (I hope we do not have to get in her smelly car again!). Tall Girl says that Mommy is not here after all, and she looks sad. But as soon as Pink Lips Lady leaves (*Good riddance—she's not our sort of person at all, is she, Quentin?*), Tall Girl says, "Come on, we have to find Vic."

I pick up my backpack and Quiet Girl takes my hand and we follow. Tall Girl walks through a door and peeks behind curtains, as if it is a game of hide-and-seek, and on the fifth curtain she makes a happy sound and pulls the curtain back and I see Loud Boy sitting up in bed and he looks happy to see us.

"Hey, Q-man!" His voice is loud again, but it does not bother me as much. Loud Boy throws his arms out to the sides, nearly hitting Tall Girl, and says, "We finished the quest! Did you see your mom?"

Tall Girl makes a noise (*if you talk like a barnyard animal, you might just turn into one!*) and says, "We've got to get out of here."

Loud Boy says, "Now? Why?"

There are still a lot of wires attached to Loud Boy, but he does not look broken anymore, so Ambulance Man was right. Loud Boy and Tall Girl start to disconnect the wires. There is a needle in his hand, and they are about to take it out, but I say, "No!"

"What?" They both look at me.

"Blood," I say.

"Oh." Tall Girl makes a face. "I guess we'll have to take it with us, then."

She grabs a bag off a metal stand and hands it to Loud Boy, who says, "What am I supposed to do with this?"

"Carry it. Can you walk?"

Loud Boy stands up and says, "Yeah, sure. I feel fine."

"Good. Let's go." Tall Girl tells us all to walk "quickly and quietly," and we go out through a different door.

"What's up?" Loud Boy asks, and Tall Girl says,

"Shh! C'mon, dummy. The quest isn't over yet," and Loud Boy says, "Now you're talking!" but more quietly.

We walk through more doors and then we are in the parking lot and I see the smelly car and I stop because I do not want to go in the car. Tall Girl says, "What's wrong?" and I say, "Smelly car," and after a second they all laugh and Loud Boy says, "Oh yeah, Q, that car totally stinks," and Tall Girl looks back at the hospital and says, "We have to hurry."

"Hurry where?" Loud Boy asks.

"It's a surprise," she says.

"I thought you didn't like surprises," Loud Boy says.

"I've changed my mind."

We follow Tall Girl back to the street and Quiet Girl takes my hand again and we start to walk (*quickly and quietly!*) away from the hospital. I look back once, just in case Tall Girl was wrong, but she is not. Mommy is not there. Mommy is somewhere else now.

# FOURTEEN

## VIC

Man, it's been a weird day. I still felt kind of out of it as Nevaeh hustled us away from the hospital, but whatever they put in that IV bag was helping. I looked like a big weirdo carrying it around, though.

We ended up on a street that looked a lot like the one where I passed out. The doctor at the hospital had given me a long lecture about remembering to take my meds, and I was like, "Dude, I was on a quest! Can't blame a guy for being busy," and he gave me a funny look and said, "Then keep a couple of them with you at all times."

Yeah, whatever. I'd told him that I'd try harder (and I will, I swear). But I was totally fine now. Better than fine. I felt practically indestructible, like if I pushed off the ground hard enough I might actually be able to fly.

"You could feel some euphoria," the doctor had said,

without explaining what that was. "So take it easy."

Yeah, right. Not so easy when Nevaeh was going, like, a hundred miles an hour. Mara was practically running to keep up, and Quentin's face was bright red, like he might be the next of us to pass out. Nevaeh didn't stop until we were really far away from the hospital, and even then she kept checking back. I couldn't see a tail following us, though, and I'd definitely be able to spot one.

"I think we're okay," Nevaeh said, and it was so much like something out of a movie that I felt even more "euphoria."

"So what's the surprise?" I asked.

"We're taking a little field trip," Nevaeh said, walking again.

"Where?" I ask.

"You'll see."

She seemed different somehow, not her usual grumpy self at all. There were big holes in the knees of her jeans, and she had bandages on her knees and elbows. I'd almost forgotten about how she ran out into traffic. Seeing the bandages gave me a funny tightness in my chest. "Did you get hit?"

"What?" she asked, even though she obviously knew what I was talking about.

"By a car," I said. Duh.

"Just a little," she said dismissively, which I gotta

admit was pretty impressive. I mean, I had no idea that Nevaeh was so tough. Come to think of it, she would probably make a pretty good operative.

"Cool," I said. She threw me a look, and I said, "What? You're the one who ran into traffic."

"I didn't mean to," she said, and I knew exactly what she meant. I remembered lying on the sidewalk, feeling like someone else had taken over my body. Of course, that was because I forgot to take my meds (for three days! Which seriously shouldn't have been a big deal). Nevaeh doesn't need meds, but sometimes you couldn't control yourself—things just happened.

I glanced back at Quentin. He was holding Mara's hand, plodding along like usual. I leaned in and asked, "What about his mom?"

Nevaeh's lips pressed together, and she shook her head. "She's gone."

I almost asked where she went, but then I understood. Gone, as in *gone* gone. Gone forever. Not coming back. It felt like someone popped a balloon inside of me, and all the euphoria came hissing out. "He doesn't know?"

"They told him, but I think that maybe he didn't completely understand." Nevaeh looked tired, like someone had popped her euphoria balloon too.

The IV bag was almost empty, and I really wished I could just dump it. "So now what?"

"So now we go to the beach."

"For real?" I asked, startled.

Nevaeh nodded. "Might as well. After today, we probably won't be allowed to leave the house for anything but school." She glanced at me. "That's gonna make it a lot harder to do your missions, I'll bet."

I couldn't tell if she was teasing. I shrugged. "I'm thinking of taking a break from the missions for a while."

"Yeah?" She looked surprised.

"Sure. I mean, Q's going to need me, right? For this whole thing with his mom."

Nevaeh stared at me for a minute, then she said, "You're a good kid, Vic."

"I know," I said. "And you're a pretty good sister." I waited for her to correct me with "foster sister," but she didn't. She just grinned.

# NEVAEH

Let me tell you about the beach, in case you've never been. The sand is a lot hotter than you'd think; we took off our shoes to walk across it, and halfway to the water ended up running and yelling because it was burning our feet. I guess that sounds kind of bad, but it wasn't; hot sand might be my favorite kind of pain ever. Especially when we reached the water, and a wave crashed over my feet and my jeans got soaked (making the cuts on my knees sting). But it tickled, too, and the water cooled my feet instantly. I was laughing and Vic and Mara were laughing and even Quentin started making that weird barking sound again.

We stood in the waves getting completely soaked, trying to hop over the foam. The beach was filled with colors, which looked even brighter against the sand: bathing suits and umbrellas, and it was all dazzling, like that moment in *The Wizard of Oz* when the movie switched from black and white to color, making you realize that you've been living in a drab, depressing world all along.

Vic's IV bag was empty, so we carefully took out the needle. It didn't bleed too much, and I used a couple of loose Band-Aids that I kept in my bag for emergencies to patch him up. He said he'd never felt better, and his color was good again, so I decided we were fine to stay a little longer.

Vic announced, "We are castaways on a desert island! We must go in search of food. There must be clams out here, or . . . hey, maybe we can make a fishing pole out of this!"

I looked at the piece of driftwood he was holding up triumphantly, then dug in my pocket and took out my emergency money. We bought hot dogs smothered in onions and mustard, and ate them on a bench by a water fountain. There was just enough cash left for four ice-cream cones, and we walked down the beach as we ate them. The ice cream dripped all over Mara's and Quentin's faces and hands, but I didn't say a word, just grinned back at them.

Afterward, we washed up in the water. Vic splashed me, and I splashed him back, and then we were all splashing each other and I couldn't stop laughing. I swear I've never laughed so much in my entire life.

The afternoon shadows lengthened, and it started to cool down. We decided to build a sandcastle. Vic called it "the most awesomest sandcastle ever built," and I have to admit it was pretty good, especially considering the fact that we didn't have any buckets or shovels. While Quentin and Mara went up and down the beach looking for shells and seaweed to decorate it, Vic and me sat down where the sand was slightly damp from the waves. I burrowed my feet in until they were completely buried.

"We are castaways, you know," Vic said out of nowhere.

"This beach isn't exactly deserted," I snorted. "Look around."

"Yeah, but we're the other kind of castaway. Like the things people throw away, get it?"

I looked at him. There was a deep sadness underneath his words, even though he'd tried to say it casually. "Castaways are survivors, right?"

"Right," he said after a second.

"So maybe it's not such a bad thing."

"Maybe." A long beat, then he said, "I'm sorry."

"For what?"

"Taking off this morning was stupid." He threw the last bite of his ice-cream cone onto the sand. Without meeting my eyes, he muttered, "The quest was stupid."

"No, it wasn't," I said reflexively. "I should've helped you."

He looked at me. "Seriously?"

"Yeah," I said. After a minute, I added, "You're still an idiot, though."

He laughed, and I laughed with him. Quentin and Mara were coming back, their hands full of beach detritus. The cuffs of Mara's pajamas were wet and sandy, and her cheeks were flushed. She was beaming from ear to ear. Quentin wasn't smiling, but he looked as happy as I'd ever seen him.

Which only made this even harder. *There's never going to be a good time*, I thought. Still, I didn't even know where to begin.

As if guessing what I was about to do, Vic reached for my hand and gave it a squeeze. I threw him a grateful look, then called out, "Quentin! Come here for a second."

Quentin trotted over to us.

"Want to sit down?" I offered.

Obligingly, he plunked down next to me. His hair was mussed, his clothes rumpled. He finally looked like a kid, not a miniature grown-up. I cleared my throat and said, "Um, so you know how we couldn't find your mom at the hospital?"

He gazed at me flatly, like a dog awaiting a command.

"Well, I talked to Ms. Judy—"

"Smelly car," he said solemnly. "Pink lips."

Vic started cracking up. I threw him a "be serious" look and said, "Right. So anyway . . . Ms. Judy said that your mom was in the hospital because she was really sick. And sometimes when people get really sick, they, um . . ." I struggled for words—what was the right thing to say? If the fact that his mother was dead hadn't penetrated when they first told him, how could I help him understand?

"Mr. Pebbles," Quentin said, out of nowhere.

"Who the heck is Mr. Pebbles?" Vic asked.

"Gone to a better place," Quentin said.

*Mr. Pebbles must've been a pet that died*, I realized. "Right, yeah. Like Mr. Pebbles, your mom went to a better place." It sounded hollow; I wished that I actually believed in something like that.

"My mom is in a better place too," Vic piped up. He didn't say anything about his dad, which made me feel guilty all over again.

"So's mine," I said. "And it's hard, but . . . you get used to it. Right?"

I looked to Vic for support. After a long moment, he slowly nodded and said, "Yeah. But it's still okay to miss them, and think about them."

"Exactly," I said. "So your mom is still kind of with you, as long as you think about her. Does that make sense?"

Quentin looked skeptical, as if debating whether we were telling the truth.

"I'm sorry, Quentin," I said, reaching out and touching the sand next to him. "Really sorry."

Mara was scrambling around the castle, sticking shells on the turrets. A seagull flew past overhead, squawking. Quentin sat for a few minutes, staring at the water. Then he said, "Mommy is gone."

"Yeah, dude," Vic said sympathetically. "It totally sucks. Sorry."

Quentin took off his backpack. He unzipped it slowly, then dug around inside for a minute before pulling out a giant R2-D2 alarm clock.

"Man, no wonder that thing is so heavy!" Vic said. "That's pretty sweet, Q."

Quentin examined the clock carefully, as if checking for damage. Then he got up and walked over to the sandcastle and rested it carefully on top. Mara regarded it appraisingly for a moment, then decorated the area around it with shells, and draped long strands of seaweed around it.

We sat there for a long time as the tide came in. Mara scampered across the beach chasing birds, but Quentin, Vic, and me watched the waves approach. Before long, they reached the edges of our castle. We stayed there, silent and still, as they crept closer. A large one swept in and sucked away the turrets on the far side. The next wave flooded the moat. Before long, water was lapping at R2-D2's base.

Vic said, "You sure about this, Q-man?"

Quentin nodded. Mara came and sat beside him, taking his hand. The sun started to set over the ocean, scattering brilliant colors across the sky. A chill crept in, and I wrapped my arms around myself for warmth. A breeze blew back my hair. The beach had gradually emptied, until the four of us were basically alone.

Water roared in and tipped R2-D2 over; he lay on his back helplessly, like an upended beetle.

The next wave sent him skittering toward the shore-line, leaving deep grooves in the sand.

The one after that dragged him into the frothing breakers, which swallowed him completely. As the sky shifted to darker shades of blue and black, R2-D2 swirled in the waves, occasionally bobbing up to the surface as if saying goodbye.

## QUENTIN

I like the beach. It is surprising how many things I like now. I like buses and trains and Ferris wheels. I like Loud Boy and Tall Girl, and I like Quiet Girl best of all.

On the train, I ask Vic if the quest is over now and he says, "Yeah, man."

That makes me sad. I like quests, too. I think that it would be nice if we had a medal ceremony like at the end of *Star Wars: Episode IV—A New Hope* with music and people clapping and Princess Leia smiling. But maybe not all quests end like that. Maybe sometimes they end at the beach, and that is nice too.

Mommy is gone (*to a better place*) like Mr. Pebbles. My tummy feels bad, like when I ate too fast and Mommy had to give me nasty pink syrup. I wonder if pink syrup will make my tummy feel better this time. I tell Tall Girl that my tummy hurts and she says, "Mine does too, Quentin," and then Quiet Girl squeezes my hand and that helps a little.

It takes a long time to get back to the brown house (a train and two buses and lots and lots of walking, so much that my feet start to hurt as much as my tummy).

It is dark when we arrive, and Porch Lady is there, and so is Pink Lips Lady, and they are very angry, mostly at Tall Girl. They ask a lot of questions, but Tall Girl does not say anything and then Loud Boy says, "Lay off my sister, Smelly Car Lady!" When he says that, Tall Girl starts to laugh and I realize it is time to make jokes again, so I say, "Shred fat sue fast!" and then everyone is laughing except for the ladies—they still look angry.

Porch Lady says, "Go to bed, we talk more in morning," and so we go upstairs and brush our teeth and put on pajamas and turn off the light.

I still have sand on my feet, now it is on the sheets and it is nice, like the beach came home with us because it likes us too. Loud Boy says, "Hey, Q. Sorry again about your mom, dude."

And I say, "Thank you," because *good manners are always in fashion!* I am sorry, too, because I cannot go with Mommy to the better place (Tall Girl says I will someday, but not for a long time). A better place sounds nice, a place with Mommy and Mr. Pebbles and R2-D2 now, too. I bet there is a beach in the better place, and a Ferris wheel, and hot dogs and ice cream. And Dora, because that will make Quiet Girl happy.

I wonder if Mommy would be happy here, in a bunk bed. It is really not so dangerous if you are careful, and sometimes it is nice to have a person sleep above you, even if they make a lot of noise. It is much nicer than the hospital. It is also nicer than the smelly car and the angry dog place and the loud street.

Something occurs to me and I ask Loud Boy, "Is

this a better place?"

At first I think he is asleep, because he does not answer for a long time. "No," he says. "But it's a pretty good place."

And I think he is right.

# FIFTEEN

## VIC

Man, Mrs. K and Ms. Judy were ticked off when we got back. I'd never seen either of them so angry. They both started yelling at us, and then they yelled at each other for a while, then they sent us to bed and kept arguing.

I waited until I heard the door slam behind Ms. Judy, then I went downstairs. Mrs. K was sitting at the kitchen table. She still looked really mad, but tired, too. "Back to bed, Vic," she snapped when I came in.

"It was my fault," I said. "Nevaeh didn't do anything. Please don't send her away."

Mrs. K looked like she was about to yell again, but then her shoulders sagged. She waved at the cup in front of her and said in her funny accent, "You want tea?"

It was so weird for her to offer me anything. I couldn't tell whether that was good or bad; maybe she was going to send us all away. Which would totally suck, especially now that we'd basically become real brothers and sisters.

Warily, I sat down across from her. Mrs. K was old, with thin, straggly blond hair and a lot of wrinkles from when she used to smoke (at least, that's what she said they were from). She had squinty blue eyes, and her teeth were crooked. At home she always wore baggy, faded sweat suits that were probably older than me. She actually made Q look stylish in comparison. There was a picture in the living room of her and Mr. K where she was younger and prettier, but it was black-and-white, so it must've been taken a really, really long time ago.

She poured me some tea from an old-fashioned teapot. It wasn't very warm, but I added a few scoops of sugar and it tasted okay.

"Careful, not so much," she said. "You still sick."

"I feel fine now," I said.

"Good."

We sat there for a few minutes. It almost felt like she was a real mom for a change, worrying about how I was feeling and giving me tea before bed. I swallowed hard, remembering the hallucination I'd had earlier, because that's what it was, I'd decided. All that talk about Q's mom had made me miss my own so much that when my brain shorted out, it produced her. I'd like to think it was something else, that she'd appeared for real. But that was imaginary stuff, and on the way home I'd decided I was done with all that. The rest of them needed me now—especially Q—and I couldn't let them down.

Mrs. K was staring into her cup. The only sounds were the grandfather clock in the hall and Mara snoring upstairs; for a little kid, she made a lot of noise when she slept.

"So, like I was saying," I said, gripping the cup in both hands, "it wasn't Nevaeh's fault."

"Nevaeh is good girl," Mrs. K finally said.

"Yeah, she's the best," I agreed. Somehow, I had to convince her to let Nevaeh stay. We had a good thing going here—even better after today. If she sent Nevaeh away, it would turn bad pretty darn fast.

Mrs. K eyed me appraisingly. "You know why I do this? Take children in?"

She said "children" funny, like it had three syllables. "Because you like kids?" I ventured.

She cocked her head to the side. "My husband, he love children. And I could not give him any. So we decide—he decide—we take in children no one wants. Give them a home. That make him happy. Make the children happy." She looked exhausted all of a sudden, and sad. "Then he die. I still take children. But maybe I don't do such a good job."

I was tempted to argue, but it would be a lie. She

wasn't exactly in the running for foster mother of the year. Maybe she'd been different when her husband was alive. She probably missed him.

I'd never thought about it before, but Mrs. K must be pretty lonely. She didn't have any friends or relatives, at least none that I'd ever seen. When she was here, she just hung out alone, watching TV or sleeping. She was crying less lately, but sometimes at night I could still hear her sobs under the noise of the TV. "I lost my mom," I offered.

"I know," she said, looking puzzled.

"And it totally sucks," I said. "So it must suck for you that your husband died."

"Yes," she agreed. "It sucked."

The way she said "sucked" was too funny—I couldn't help it, I started laughing. After a second, her eyes crinkled and she laughed too. Quietly, because neither of us wanted to wake the others.

"You good boy, Vic."

"Nah," I said, taking another sip of tea. "I mess stuff up. Not on purpose, though."

"Well, is life," she said with another heavy sigh. "Everyone mess up."

"You have to keep trying, though, right? To be good?"

Mrs. K gave me another long look. "Yes, is good to try."

"So Nevaeh can stay?" I asked hopefully.

Mrs. K looked confused. "Why you think Nevaeh leaving?"

"Well, because of Mario," I said. "Plus Silvia, and Anya . . ."

"Silvia and Anya went back with families," Mrs. K said. "And Mario, well. Mario was good boy, but he was also trouble."

I couldn't disagree with that. I frowned. "So you don't get rid of kids when they become teenagers?"

Mrs. K looked shocked. "What? No, Vic."

"Oh," I said. "Cool." Now I felt kind of dumb. I tried to remember who'd told me that—was it Mario? Probably. Maybe he hadn't been such a great guy after all. I realized something. "Hey, so that means we're all staying together!"

Mrs. K sighed and shook her head. "I don't know, Vic. Ms. Judy think maybe I should not foster children anymore." She frowned at the tea leaves lining the rim of her cup. "Now she come every week to check."

"No problem," I said confidently.

Mrs. K threw me a look. "No?"

"Nope," I said. "We'll tell her you're the best foster mom ever. Trust me, I know Ms. Judy. She'll forget all about this in a few months. She's got a ton of cases anyway; she's always saying she can barely keep up."

She was still shaking her head. "You sweet boy,

Vic. But you deserve better. You all do."

"Trust me, Mrs. K, this is the best place for us." Thinking of Quentin, I added, "There's no better place, seriously. We love it here."

She looked doubtful, so I added, "Honestly, I know today was, like, not great, and we shouldn't have run off like that. But it made me realize something. I really, really like living here. I like Nevaeh and Mara and Q and you. And I don't want to have to leave. I don't want any of us to go."

Tears spiked in my eyes. I swallowed hard to fight them back, but it didn't work. Mrs. K's face softened, and she gave my hand a firm squeeze. "Okay, Vic. We try."

"Really?" I sniffled. When she nodded, I said, "You won't regret this, Mrs. K. I swear it."

"No swearing," she said, jabbing a finger at me, but I could tell she was kidding. First Q started making jokes, now Mrs. K? We were turning into a bunch of comedians. "Now to bed."

"Sure." I swiped my hand across my face to dry it, then got up and collected both of our cups. I rinsed them out in the sink and put them in the dishwasher so Nevaeh wouldn't have to deal with them in the morning. As I passed Mrs. K, I gave her a quick, awkward peck on the cheek. I'm not sure why, it just seemed like the right thing to do.

Looking surprised, she patted my hand and said, "Have good dreams, Vic."

## NEVAEH

"Vic, hurry up! You're going to make us all late!" I hollered up the stairs.

He came catapulting down, nearly knocking me over, his hair still wet from the shower. "Sorry," he said breathlessly. "Couldn't find my homework."

"Did you—"

"Yup, took my pill," he said, pulling on his backpack. Quentin and Mara were already waiting by the door.

"Good." I had to admit, Vic had surprised me over the past few months. He was still hyper and annoying, but he'd actually been helping me cook and clean up. He and Quentin were building some sort of elaborate Star Wars village in their room out of old plastic food containers; they spent hours in there, heads bent together. Mara painted the buildings as they finished them, wielding a tiny brush with almost unsettling intensity.

I still kept waiting for the ax to fall. The morning after the "quest" ended, I awoke to the sound of pots and pans being banged around downstairs, and my gut immediately clenched. I'd barely slept the night before, knowing what was coming.

But when we came down, Mrs. K was in the kitchen making scrambled eggs. There was toast, too, and orange juice already poured. I pulled out my chair with a sense of dread—two hot breakfasts in one week was unprecedented, and probably not a good sign. But Mrs. K didn't say a word about the day before; she just told me to eat my eggs. Reluctantly, I choked down a few bites, then went upstairs and packed my battered suitcase.

But Ms. Judy never showed up, and Mrs. K acted like our trip to Torrance had never happened. Days passed, then weeks, and still . . . nothing. In fact, Mrs. K seemed a lot happier. She watched TV with us at night, she started making dinner again, and she did more of the laundry and cleaning, too. I hardly ever heard her crying anymore.

It was mystifying, like during the night someone had replaced her with someone else. When I asked Vic what was up, he shrugged and said, "Dunno. I guess my charm finally won her over."

Which was obviously not the case. But Vic claimed he'd been lying about the high school thing just to get back at me for what I'd said about his dad. I didn't totally believe him, but summer had come and gone, and I was still here. So that was something.

"Let's go, or we'll be late for school," I said, herding

them out the door. Quentin was looking a lot cooler these days, thanks to Vic's fashion advice. Today he was wearing basketball shorts and a Star Wars T-shirt. The kid was seriously obsessed with Star Wars; it was hard to believe he'd ever been quiet, because now it was hard to get him to shut up about it. He had an aide at school who he really liked, and that seemed to make a big difference; he hadn't had a freak-out in months. He and Vic spent most of their time pretending to be Luke Skywalker and Han Solo; for Halloween this year, they wanted Mara to dress up as Princess Leia when we went trick-or-treating so they'd all match. "And you can be Obi-Wan," Vic said.

"I'm supposed to be an old white guy? No thanks." I snorted.

"But you're totally our Obi-Wan," he said. "Like, the force is strong with you, y'know?"

I didn't admit it, but that *was* kind of flattering. I'd decided to go as Shuri from *Black Panther* instead, which made Vic roll his eyes and say, "Dude, wrong movie universe," but the costume was on sale and it looked awesome on me, so I told him he'd have to deal with it.

"Are we going to the beach this weekend?" Vic asked, balancing on the thin wall next to the bus stop. Quentin awkwardly climbed up behind him, arms thrown out for balance.

"Get down, both of you," I said automatically. "I'm *so* not going to the emergency room again." It was kind of cute that the two of them were inseparable now. "Brothers from another mother," like Vic kept saying.

"So are we?" Vic asked, hopping down. Quentin descended more carefully, thank God, because he was turning out to be even more accident-prone than Vic.

"Maybe," I said. "If you do all your chores." I was lying, actually; I'd already packed a bag with sunblock and towels and sand toys. Mrs. K had even gotten the day off work so she could come too.

"I like the beach," Mara said softly. She was speaking more English these days; her teacher said she'd probably be fluent by Christmas.

I gave her hand a squeeze. "I do too, sweetheart."

"Yo, sis!" Vic yelled out. "Check it!" He did a roll across the grass next to the sidewalk and landed on his side, pretending to aim a laser gun at something behind me. "Cover me, Luke!"

Quentin brought out his own fake laser gun, and the two of them made ridiculous "Pyoo, pyoo, pyoo" noises. I sighed. *Boys.*

"All right, *mi familia*," Vic said as we approached the school. "Fist bumps all around."

He held out his fist. I gave it a reluctant tap. Mara and Quentin hit it with more enthusiasm.

"Remember," I said, "I have yearbook today after

school, so you'll all have to hang out in the yard until four. Got it?"

"Got it, sis!" Vic threw me a clumsy salute, then raised his arm and said, "C'mon, Luke!"

The two of them raced toward the front door like they were being chased, nearly bowling over Mrs. Colbourne. She yelled at them to slow down, but they kept going until they vanished inside.

"We are one crazy family," Mara said, shaking her head.

She sounded so adult, it made me laugh. "Yeah," I agreed. "We sure are."

# AUTHOR'S NOTE

The foster care system in the United States (and its failures) is a very personal and important issue to me. Through my work as a court-appointed special advocate in the LA foster care system, and as a youth mentor for the LifeWorks program, I've personally witnessed the strengths and weaknesses of how we care for some of society's most vulnerable children. In this book, I wanted to lay bare the inadequacies of that system in a format that's appropriate for children, illustrating the very real challenges that foster children confront. There's obviously no one singular foster care experience, but Nevaeh, Vic, Quentin, and Mara are composites of real case studies.

Los Angeles has the nation's largest child welfare system[1], comprised of roughly 30,000 children—a number that's simply staggering. While the goal is to reunite foster children with their birth families whenever possible, a quarter of the youth who entered foster care in 2012 spent twenty-nine months or more in foster homes[2]. The "Welcome Center" that Nevaeh described in such disparaging terms was a real place—one of many, in fact—and older children were more likely to experience extended stays there because so few people were willing to house them[3]. In 2016, those centers were shuttered after

1. www.lacounty.gov/residents/family-services/children-families
2. www.latimes.com/local/countygovernment/la-me-adv-foster-parents-20160327-story.html
3. www.latimes.com/local/california/la-me-adv-foster-overflow-20150301-story.html

a lawsuit alleged that they amounted to illegal foster care facilities; rather than the maximum twenty-four-hour stay mandated by state law, children were frequently placed there for weeks[4]. Since the centers closed, care of these children has been outsourced to private contractors, the results of which are decidedly mixed. In light of all that, Nevaeh's willingness to go to such extraordinary lengths to stay at Mrs. K's house, despite its glaring imperfections, is understandable.

Almost half the foster children in LA end up homeless or incarcerated once they age out of the system. Only 58 percent of LA foster children even graduate from high school, never mind college, so Nevaeh's life plan is truly impressive considering the odds she's fighting against[5].

Sadly, the kind of abuse she describes experiencing in previous foster homes is also all too prevalent[6]. The federal government has given California particularly bad marks on monitoring the well-being of children in foster care. In some cases, state officials took more than a year to investigate complaints of abuse or neglect, failing to notify investigators of serious sexual abuse allegations and neglecting follow-up visits to determine if cases had been resolved. Those failures left many children in foster home situations that ranged from negligent to downright dangerous[7].

On top of that, the number of available foster homes in LA dropped 52 percent between 2005 and 2015[8], validating

4.  www.latimes.com/local/countygovernment/la-me-foster-care-last
    -resort-20160301-story.html
5.  www.kids-alliance.org/facts-stats/
6.  www.latimes.com/local/countygovernment/la-me-inspection-backlog
    -20140913-story.html
7.  www.dailynews.com/2017/09/28/california-earns-poor-marks-on
    -monitoring-the-welfare-of-foster-children/
8.  www.chronicleofsocialchange.org/news-2/foster-parent-recruitment
    -crisis-1-county-zip-code/23551

Nevaeh's fears that Mrs. K might consider leaving the foster program, throwing her and her foster siblings back into limbo. By 2013, there were 6,300 children to place, and only 3,440 foster homes; a lot of foster families bailed out of the system because of low reimbursement and inadequate support[9].

That's why Judy allows Mrs. K to continue fostering children, despite the fact that she's clearly an imperfect foster parent. Judy's workload doesn't help matters either; social workers in the LA foster care system are overwhelmed by unreasonable caseloads, assigned nearly twice as many as their colleagues in New York City[10]. In spite of that, I'm constantly awestruck by the devotion to these kids demonstrated by every social worker I've come across. There's a huge team of people ranging from foster parents to children's attorneys to social workers who work tirelessly to improve the lives of foster children. In my opinion, they're the great unsung heroes of our time.

Quentin's experience demonstrates the particular challenges of finding a foster home for someone on the autism spectrum. In LA County, the shortage of foster beds means it might take a hundred phone calls to place a child with any special need—and that group includes teenagers, infants, and siblings, not just youngsters with physical or mental challenges[11]. Yet nearly half the foster children in LA have learning disabilities or delays[12]; so it's easy to see how finding appropriate homes is a nearly impossible endeavor. While obviously

9. https://blueprint.ucla.edu/feature/los-angeles-foster-children-and-those -who-care-for-them/
10. www.newsroom.ucla.edu/stories/los-angeles-foster-children-and -those-who-care-for-them
11. https://blueprint.ucla.edu/feature/los-angeles-foster-children-and -those-who-care-for-them/
12. www.kids-alliance.org/facts-stats/

Quentin would need a classroom aide, especially as a child on the autism spectrum who had previously been homeschooled, the reality is that the process to receive such an aide takes months[13]. And that's for a child with an educated, involved parent who can navigate the process. Although the LAUSD has been trying to streamline the process in recent years, a current teacher shortage (especially in special education) has meant that even more kids like Quentin end up slipping through the cracks[14].

I wrote this story to help kids understand the unique challenges that foster children face, and to shine a light on how we're failing them. But I hope that the reader's main takeaway is the incredible resilience of these children. The kids that I've worked with are some of the strongest and most capable people I've ever met; they've had to be, to overcome their life circumstances. And despite the tragedies that landed them in foster care, their continued optimism and desire to achieve their hopes and dreams is absolutely inspirational. I've always believed that helping one person can have an enormous impact on the world, especially when that person is a child. Volunteering as a CASA has been one of the most enriching experiences of my life, and I highly recommend it. More information on the program is here: www.casaforchildren.org.

At its heart, this is the story of four vastly different kids coming together and creating their own found family, forging a connection that helps them overcome obstacles. Like Nevaeh says, sometimes you have to rescue your own self. And Nevaeh, Quentin, Vic, and Mara manage to do just that.

---

13.  www.laparent.com/special-needs-IEP
14.  www.learningpolicyinstitute.org/product/addressing-californias
     -growing-teacher-shortage-2017-update-report